THE LONDON MURDER
MYSTERIES

Cora Harrison is the author of many successful books for children and adults. She lives on a small farm in the west of Ireland with her husband, her German Shepherd dog called Oscar and a very small white cat called Polly.

Find out more about Cora at:
www.coraharrison.com

To discover why Cora wrote
the London Murder Mysteries, head online to:
www.piccadillypress.co.uk/londonmurdermysteries

The London Murder Mysteries

The Montgomery Murder
The Deadly Fire
Murder on Stage
Death of a Chimney Sweep
The Body in the Fog
Death in Devil's Acre *(coming soon)*

THE LONDON MURDER MYSTERIES

THE BODY

IN THE FOG

CORA HARRISON

PICCADILLY PRESS • LONDON

First published in Great Britain in 2012
by Piccadilly Press Ltd,
5 Castle Road, London NW1 8PR
www.piccadillypress.co.uk

A catalogue record for this book is available
from the British Library

ISBN: 978 1 84812 169 0 (paperback)
978 1 84812 205 5 (ebook)

1 3 5 7 9 10 8 6 4 2

Printed and bound by CPI Group (UK) Ltd, Croydon, CR0 4YY
Cover design by Patrick Knowles
Cover illustration by Chris King

*For my friends Cath Thompson and Marie Neal
who inspired me to investigate the fascinating subject of
the underground rivers of London.*

CHAPTER 1

WHY KILL A BEGGAR?

Alfie saw the body just before all hell broke loose in Trafalgar Square.

It was after midnight and the streets were filled with a choking yellow fog, but there was no mistaking the fact that the man sprawled on the ground was dead.

Alfie and his cousin Jack were making their way home after a night's fishing. They stopped and stared at each other at the sight of the body. They knew who it was. As far back as they could remember, Jemmy the beggar had sat under that statue every day of his life – and now he was dead.

The next moment, there was a sudden explosion and a

whoosh of orange flames from Morley's Hotel, above the post office. All eyes on Trafalgar Square went up to the hotel balcony. Screams rang out and the foggy air was filled with a smell of smoke. Men began to yell and women to shriek. There were shouts of 'Fire! Get the fire brigade, someone!'

A minute later, two horses pulling the mail van shot out through the archway beneath the hotel. The screams on the balcony were drowned out by yells of 'Stop, thieves!', as a crowd of post office men in red uniforms came running out after the mail van.

A policeman in the centre of Trafalgar Square blew a shrill whistle. There was an answering blast from another policeman across the road. A masked man was driving the mail van, lashing the horses on, and the van almost overturned as it wheeled around the statue of King Charles, where Alfie and Jack stood beside the dead body.

A piece of paper fluttered from the hand that held the whip and fell to the ground. Alfie bent down and grabbed it and, as he looked up, the glittering eyes behind the driver's mask seemed to pierce right through him. Then there was another lash of the whip and a screech of wheels, and the mail van was gone towards the River Thames.

'Let's get out of here,' said Alfie in a low voice. He had begun to guess what was happening. He knew the man who drove the horses. That scar on the chin was unmistakable. It was Flash Harry himself.

But it was too late.

A policeman's hands gripped their collars.

CHAPTER 2

TROUBLE

The policeman had a narrow face, a massive bright red nose and a piercing gaze. His eyes moved from the dead body to the two boys. Jack shuffled his bare feet uncertainly and Alfie gazed back with as much innocence as he could manage.

'Know anything about this?' The policeman jerked his thumb at the lifeless body on the pavement, lying just beneath the enormous statue of a king mounted on a horse. 'Any idea what happened to him?' he asked.

'No, sir,' said Jack earnestly.

'Got kicked by that stone horse,' ventured Alfie and then he forgot his own joke as something about the body took his attention.

Old Jemmy looked much the same as usual, except for the huge wound on his forehead. He wore the same filthy old coat, three sizes too big for him and the same pair of old boots gaping wide. He had the same ginger moustache and the same ginger beard. And yet, there was something different. Alfie moved a little closer and peered at the face of the dead man. Yes, he thought, that's strange. But he said nothing.

The policeman did not wait. It was more important to deal with live robbers than dead beggar men, so he released the boys and joined the crowd of whistle-blowing, truncheon-waving police who were charging after the stolen mail van. A few shots rang out, but there were no answering shots.

'I reckon that was Flash Harry and his mob raiding the post office. Let's get out of here,' said Alfie to his cousin.

'And leave *him*?' Jack indicated the body on the ground.

Alfie shrugged. 'Why not? None of our business! The law has seen him. Up to the policeman, now. We're lucky that he had the robbery to occupy him – otherwise we'd be arrested on suspicion of murder.'

'You think someone murdered him?' Jack was reluctant to move. He bent down over the body. 'He's been here a while – look at the way the water has run off his body and left little bits of ice all around him. Funny, that! There ain't been no rain – just fog. Do you reckon it were the post office robbers that killed him, Alfie?'

'Don't know, don't care,' grunted Alfie. 'Probably a drunken fight. You know Jemmy. He'd fight with his own shadow.'

'He didn't drink,' said Jack. 'You remember the time he rescued me from that drunk cracksman? Well, he told me then that he hadn't had a drink for five years. He said that drink was the undoing of him. He told me that the aunt who brought him up was always drunk and she taught him to drink and that's what landed him on the streets. He used to warn me to stay out of public houses.'

Alfie didn't answer. He was busy looking at the piece of paper that had been dropped by the masked robber. It puzzled him. The paper was thick and very white and the edges were scalloped in gold. Costs money, paper like that, he thought. Not the sort of thing that you'd expect robbers or cracksmen to have. There was a sort of mark woven into the paper – letters, were they, perhaps a G and an O twisted together? – that he could only see when he held it up to the nearby gas lamp. It seemed to be a note, though it was not addressed to anyone. The signature at the bottom of the page was just a scrawl, but the message was the strange bit.

Right at the top of the piece of paper was the drawing of a clock face. The hands were set to twelve o'clock. Beside it was drawn a slice of moon. Midnight, thought Alfie.

And that was all. No words – nothing.

Alfie's mind worked quickly. He had learnt to read at the Ragged School, but many people couldn't. The raid and all the details had probably been worked out beforehand. All the robbers needed was the day and the time.

And today the message had been sent to Flash Harry to tell him that something worth stealing was going by the midnight post.

'Alfie,' said Jack urgently, 'let's get going. Look at them two men coming over. I reckon they're part of Flash Harry's mob. They're looking at us. One of them is pointing.'

Alfie acted instinctively. Hastily, he screwed up the piece of paper and shoved it into the carved stone pattern of the base beneath the statue beside them.

'Run!' he said in Jack's ear and in a minute they were dodging through a crowd of men who had just come up some steps into Trafalgar Square.

This was a good move. The men were large, tough-looking fellows, and although they allowed the two barefoot boys through, they shouted abuse in strong

Birmingham accents at the two mobsters as they tried to push their way past them. Alfie, glancing over his shoulder, saw that he and Jack might escape. The fog was thick and, once away from the gaslights of Trafalgar Square, they could lose themselves in the network of small lanes between there and the boys' home in Bow Street. They only had to cross the road to St Martin's church and then they might be safe.

But a horse-drawn bus full of uniformed policemen was blocking their way, closely followed by a second and a third. The wait seemed agonisingly long. Jack lost patience and dived between the second and third buses. Alfie followed him, and in a moment they were both running up St Martin's Lane.

By the time the last of the three buses had gone, Alfie, glancing over his shoulder, could see that only one man was still behind them. His right hand was stuck into his pocket and Alfie knew enough about gangs to guess that he had a pistol there.

'Run faster, Alfie!' Jack shouted, looking back anxiously and Alfie sprinted down the lane after his cousin.

The race was on. The penalty for losing could be death.

CHAPTER 3

HUNTED

Alfie ran as fast as he could. His heart was thudding and his chest was searingly hot as he tried to suck in more air. He and Jack were dead tired. They had both been working all night, pulling up the heavy nets full of twisting eels, carrying loaded boxes from Charlie Higgins's boat to the stalls at Hungerford market.

Down Long Acre they went. Alfie could hear the sound of Jack's bare feet slapping on the stone pavement of the street ahead of him, but then he turned into Bow Street and the noise ceased. Alfie stopped. He could run no more. He tried to draw breath, holding onto his knees while he gasped and shook and black dots danced in front of his eyes. As soon as he was able, he looked over his shoulder. The man was gaining on him. His hand had come out from his pocket. It did not hold a gun as Alfie had feared, but a gleam of light from the overhead gas lamp showed the glint of a knife blade.

The next moment, the breath was knocked from Alfie's body as the man's weight toppled him to the ground. Alfie wrestled with him like a tiger, though the man was twice his weight. But when he felt the point of the knife prick his throat, he lay quite still. Men from Flash Harry's mob would not hesitate to kill.

'What did you do with that letter?' hissed the man. He was digging into Alfie's pockets, ripping his already torn shirt wide open.

'Threw it away,' gasped Alfie.

'That's a lie,' hissed the man into his ear. The point of the knife dug in a little deeper.

It had crossed Alfie's mind to tell the truth about where he had hidden the piece of paper, but he decided against it. The mobster would probably drag him back to Trafalgar Square and knife him in a dark corner once the note was secured. *Dead men tell no tales* was the motto of most of these London mobs – and it applied just as well to dead boys.

Where was Jack? wondered Alfie despairingly and, as

soon as the thought had passed through his mind, he had his answer.

A very large and very hairy dog came flying down Bow Street, his barks changing to menacing growls as he saw his master on the ground. He seized the man's knife arm in his mouth and held it firmly, his lips stretched in a menacing snarl. He looked like a dog that would kill.

The man swore and screamed and let go of Alfie, dropping the knife to the ground. Then Jack appeared from nowhere and picked up the knife, holding it threateningly towards the villain's throat.

Slowly Alfie got to his feet. He was bruised all over and his heart still thumped. He could feel blood running down his neck but he strove to make his voice sound strong. 'Now listen, you,' he said. 'I'll give you ten seconds to get out of this place. If you're still here after that, well, this here dog of mine ain't had any supper and he's not choosy. Leg of man tastes as good to him as leg of lamb. So scarper. Let him go, Mutsy.'

Mutsy reluctantly took his teeth out of the man's sleeve, but he continued to snarl and to growl until the fellow had limped off, swearing loudly. Then he looked up at Alfie and wagged his tail.

Alfie patted the dog's head. 'Good job you managed to get ahead and send Mutsy,' said Alfie to his cousin. 'That fellow is definitely one of Flash Harry's mob. I've seen him before. They're probably the chaps that did the post office raid. Lucky I didn't take that letter with me. I'd say that Inspector Denham will be interested to have a look at it.'

Alfie was beginning to recover and his mouth watered at the thought of the sixpence or even the shilling that they might receive from their friend, Inspector Denham, for information about the post office raid.

'If it's Flash Harry's mob, I'd keep out of this business if I were you,' said Jack uneasily. 'They're a vicious lot – kill you soon as look at you.'

CHAPTER 4

THE GANG

Home for Alfie, his blind brother Sammy and his cousins Jack and Tom was a small, damp cellar down some steps from Bow Street. It was a handy place to live, near to Covent Garden market and the theatre – both good places for the boys to beg, do tricks, sing songs or even pick up a job from time to time. Somehow or other they had managed to pay the rent and find enough food to keep themselves alive in the years since Alfie's parents died.

First there had been four of them, and then, one day, a shaggy dog with large paws had followed Alfie home from Smithfield meat market and made his home with them. Now it was almost impossible to imagine how they had managed without Mutsy. He protected the boys, guided Sammy all over London's West End and did tricks which earned the gang money, feeding himself on the rats that swarmed in the old house and through the markets. Best of all, he was a great pet for the four boys who had no other living relations.

'Poor old Jemmy, the beggar man from Trafalgar Square, has been murdered,' said Jack to Sammy when they had finished laughing over how Mutsy had arrested one of Flash Harry's gang. 'Don't know who did it, but he was hit on the head with something and it knocked his brains out,' he added, looking hopefully at Sammy. Jack had a great opinion of Sammy's brains and the blind boy had solved tricky puzzles before.

'What do you think, Alfie?' Sammy turned his face towards his brother.

'Don't know, don't care,' said Alfie impatiently. 'I keep telling you, Jack. Jemmy was a quarrelsome type. He was always fighting with someone. Never liked him, myself. Yes, I know, I know, he did you a good turn once,' he continued hastily as he saw Jack open his mouth, 'but that don't alter the fact that he was a nasty fellow.'

'He wasn't a bad fellow when you got to know him,' said Jack stubbornly. 'He had no luck in life, he said. His parents died when he was seven years old and the aunt that took him was a drinker and the one that took his twin brother Ned wasn't.' Jack paused. 'I think we should do something about him. Mutsy liked him as well.'

Alfie shrugged his shoulders. It was true that the big dog had been devoted to Jemmy for some reason, wagging his tail madly whenever he caught sight or smell of the beggar man.

'Well, let Mutsy look into the crime, then,' he said. 'There you are, Mutsy, your first case. If you find the murderer, we'll put a badge on you.'

'PC Mutsy, the rat hunter,' said Tom. 'Anyway, why was that fellow from Flash Harry's mob chasing Alfie?'

Jack told the story of the raid and how the mail van had been stolen while everyone was distracted by the fire at Morley's Hotel, and how Alfie had picked up the piece of paper. Meanwhile, Alfie was thinking about the piece of paper that he had hidden in the base of the statue of King Charles. Why was it so valuable to the thieves? Why did they go to the lengths of chasing him through the streets of London in order to get it back?

'So the paper was to say what time to start the raid?' said Sammy, as if reading his brother's thoughts. 'Flash Harry can't read so he would need a message in pictures.' He paused. 'But the raid had already happened, so why would he need to hold on to a bit of paper?'

'Dunno,' said Alfie. And then an idea came into his head. He remembered something about Flash Harry and, funnily enough, it was old Jemmy the beggar who had told him it. His words echoed in Alfie's mind: *Flash Harry keeps out of trouble because he has a hold on so many people. He'll collect evidence and keep it until he has a use for someone and then threaten to use it against them if he needs them. Blackmail, that's what it's called.*

So that was why Flash Harry sent one of his mob after me, thought Alfie. 'I'd say that Flash Harry wanted to keep the note,' he said, 'so that he could blackmail the geezer who sent it. Might be someone who works in the post office, maybe even a high-up bloke who would know that something valuable was being sent by the midnight post. Maybe I'll go and talk to Inspector Denham in the morning.'

'So we have a new mystery to solve.' Sammy had a note of satisfaction in his voice.

'And even if you get nothing from Inspector Denham, we've got something out of that business tonight,' said Tom cheerfully. He picked up the man's weapon from the mantelpiece above the fire and turned it around in his hand, watching the firelight flash from the sharp blade. 'Good knife,' he said admiringly.

'So it is,' said Alfie, taking it from him. 'Feel the edge of that, Sammy, carefully now. I'll just touch it to your finger.'

'Knife like that would shave you if you had a beard,' said Sammy, his sensitive finger feeling the razor-sharp blade.

Alfie frowned. That word 'shave' reminded him of something. He glanced across at Jack. Jack was a good fellow who had just saved Alfie's life by running ahead and releasing Mutsy from the cellar. He had a disappointed look on his face now – he was upset about Jemmy's murder and wanted to talk about that, not the post office raid. Alfie decided to try out the puzzle about Jemmy on Sammy.

Sammy Sykes was eleven years old and he had been blind from the age of two. *He has other gifts,* the boys' grandfather used to say whenever his daughter wailed about her son's blindness. And that was true. Sammy was gifted. He sang beautifully, could memorise any song and reach the highest notes without effort. He also had a brain as sharp as a razor, extraordinary hearing and an amazing ability to tell people's thoughts from the sound of their voices.

'Sammy,' said Alfie, 'what do you make of this? When Jack and me saw the dead body of old Jemmy, I had a good look at him and I saw that his beard had been trimmed. He had a ginger beard. Well, it was sort of neatened off and it seemed to be kind of shaved around the ears and along the line of the cheek.'

'Jemmy went to the barber's, had a haircut and shave and then dropped dead with the shock,' said Tom, laughing at his own wit.

'What about his hair?' asked Sammy.

'Dunno,' said Alfie. 'He was wearing that big old cap. Never saw him without it. It didn't show much in the way of hair as far as I can remember.'

Sammy shook his head slowly. 'Can't think of no reason why anyone would shave him. He must have done it himself.'

'I suppose so,' said Alfie, 'but it don't make sense.'

'He dosses down in Opium Sal's place, don't he?' said Sammy. 'Perhaps one of her customers did it to him – for a joke, like.'

'Could be,' said Alfie. Sal had an opium den down by the Hungerford Stairs. Most of the people who went there to smoke opium were so out of their minds on the drug that they might do anything, but they would be more likely to shave half his beard off, or something like that. And Jemmy was a vicious fighter who would never let those drug-crazed people do anything to him.

Alfie moved the problem to the back of his mind and looked across at his cousin. 'Jack, I don't think we can do anything about old Jemmy,' he said patiently. 'He probably had it coming to him. Do you remember him with Bert? You know, Bert the Tosher, the geezer that works in sewers. Jemmy half-killed him over that gold thing Bert found in the Tyburn sewer. And there's Opium Sal. She hated him. I think that he had some sort of hold over her. Otherwise she'd never have allowed him to doss down in her den.'

'Well, that's just it – gives us lots of suspects,' said Jack eagerly. 'And I heard someone shouting at Jemmy last night as we passed him before we went fishing – someone with a funny sort of voice, not a toff. There was a bit of an argument going on. *Don't you threaten me*, Jemmy was yelling. And then he dropped his voice a bit, but I still heard it.' Jack looked around at the other three boys and continued dramatically. '*If there's any murdering to be done, then I'll be the one to do it,* that's what Jemmy said.'

Alfie stared at Jack and then shrugged his shoulders. 'Looks like I was right when I said it were a fight. Jemmy was asking for it and he got it. There's some very tough coves around this place at night.'

CHAPTER 5

DANGER

The four boys were still asleep when Sarah knocked at the door at noon. Mutsy, though, was wide awake and stood at the door wagging his tail while his masters dressed hurriedly.

Sarah was very small and very skinny for her age. With her delicate bony face and her huge green eyes, she looked more like a child of nine than a girl of twelve. She had been a scullery maid for a few years when the boys had first met her, but had recently become a parlour maid at the White Horse Inn on Haymarket, not far from Trafalgar Square.

'Come on, sleepy heads!' she said impatiently. 'Have

you heard about the post office raid? The whole of London is talking about it. A lot of engineers from Birmingham are staying at the White Horse Inn and they were all discussing it at breakfast this morning. They saw the whole thing. There's a poster outside Bow Street police station offering a reward. Come and see.'

The boys followed Sarah immediately, Tom explaining about how Alfie and Jack had also been there on their way back from their fishing job. There was a big crowd around Bow Street police station and they had to push their way through to see the poster. Everyone was discussing the robbery excitedly. One tall woman with a basket was the centre of attention because her husband worked in the post office and she claimed he had come home with his clothes smelling of smoke.

Alfie doubted that. As far as he saw, the smoke on the balcony of the hotel had just been a diversion – something set up to scare the workers loading the mail van and make them run out into the square for those vital few minutes while Flash Harry and his mob took their places and stole the van.

'See if you can read it, Tom,' Alfie said to his youngest cousin. Tom, unlike Jack and Alfie, had not learned to read at the Ragged School; in fact he had hated it, but Jack had been patiently teaching his brother and now he had begun to make good progress. He read the poster fluently.

ROBBERY OF MAIL BAGS
AT TRAFALGAR SQUARE
YESTERDAY EVENING.
WITNESSES TO THIS CRIME ARE WANTED.
REWARD OF £10 FOR ANY INFORMATION
LEADING TO THE ARREST OF THE CRIMINALS.

Alfie hardly listened. One line danced before his eyes: REWARD OF £10. I could just do with that, he thought. He jerked his head at his gang to follow him, but did not speak until they had gone around the corner and there was no one to overhear.

'Sarah, would you do something for me? I want you to go to Trafalgar Square and get something that I hid there last night,' he said in a low voice and explained to her about the expensive piece of paper that had fallen from Flash Harry's hand as he drove the post office van across Trafalgar Square. 'I'd collect it myself, but I'm thinking that they might be watching me.'

'I'll go there straight away,' said Sarah. She paused for a moment as her quick brain raced ahead. 'Better still, I'll go in the front door to the White Horse Inn and then straight out of the back door and down the back lane to Trafalgar Square. Then if anyone's watching me, they'll think I'm just going back to work.'

'Let's all split up and go in different directions,' suggested Tom.

'Good thinking,' said Alfie. He hesitated for a moment. Money was not too flush at the moment, but he had two weeks' rent saved in the tin box and sixpence in his pocket. 'I'll get some sausages and some beer,' he continued, 'and we'll all meet back at the cellar in about an hour and have breakfast and dinner at the same time. Sam, you take Mutsy and go and do a bit of singing outside St Martin's church – you might hear something useful, seeing as it's so near the post office. Tom, you go and draw some of them mud pictures over by the Strand and keep your ears peeled. Jack, why don't you go to the fish market at Hungerford? That van last night went that way. Bet they'll all be talking about it.'

Alfie waited until his gang had disappeared one by one and then he had a look around. No one seemed to be watching so he slid in through the gate into the yard between the police station and the courthouse. There was a back door there – he remembered Inspector Denham allowing him out through it on one occasion.

Luckily the door was unlocked so Alfie went in,

passing with a shudder the room where the dead bodies were kept. Old Jemmy was probably in there, he thought, as the door to the room opened suddenly and Inspector Denham almost crashed into him.

'Lord bless me,' said the inspector, raising his bushy eyebrows. 'Where did you spring from?'

'Took the liberty of coming in by the back door, sir,' said Alfie airily. 'A man can't be too careful when he has Flash Harry on his tail.'

He thought the inspector would smile at this, but the man's bushy eyebrows drew together in a frown.

'Come in,' said Inspector Denham grimly. 'Now look here, Alfie,' he began determinedly, then stopped, looking down at Alfie's feet. 'Why don't you wear those boots I gave you?' he said in irritated tones.

'I'd spoil them in the fog and wet, sir,' said Alfie.

'Well, come and sit over here by the fire,' ordered the inspector. Alfie sat down on the small rug in front of the fire and gratefully took the handful of biscuits that was passed down to him. He warmed his frozen hands and feet, nibbled quietly at the biscuits and waited for the inspector to speak.

'You're right, of course,' said Inspector Denham after a minute. 'This does seem to be a Flash Harry job. There's somebody else involved though. We all know Flash Harry.'

He comes into London, does a job, hides out somewhere, then disappears down into the country or else goes abroad. One of these days we'll catch him – find his hideout and clap him in irons. But this time it's different.'

Inspector Denham paused, straightened the papers on his desk, and then started to speak again, his voice so low that Alfie had to strain his ears to hear it. It was almost as though the policeman was talking to himself, sorting out his own thoughts, perhaps.

'You see, Alfie,' he said. 'Very few people knew that a consignment of jewels was being sent to Amsterdam in Holland last night. There was nothing to alert Flash Harry or any of the crowd that he hangs out with. And the decision was only taken at the last moment to send them by the midnight post. Only the top men at the jewellers and a few people at the post office knew of that plan. How did Flash Harry get to know about this?'

Inspector Denham didn't appear to expect an answer to this and Alfie said nothing. He was thinking hard. He decided not to mention the dropped piece of paper. It would be best to solve the problem first, and the drawing of the clock and the moon still did not make sense to him.

'But we do have one lead,' continued the inspector, 'and perhaps this is something that you can help me with. That old beggar man was savagely killed last night –

apparently just before the robbery took place. Now, he must have known something. There is no reason, otherwise, for him to have been murdered. Keep away from Flash Harry and his mob, Alfie, but if you could bring me any information about the beggar man, well, I'll make it worth your while.'

The inspector rose to his feet, fished in his pocket, produced a shilling and handed it to Alfie. 'Here's something to be going on with,' he said. 'Now I'll let you out the back door – you might as well go the way you came.'

Inspector Denham did not speak again until they were at the back door and, to Alfie's relief, did not take him into the room where the dead bodies lay. But when Alfie stood on the cobbled yard, the inspector looked at him in a worried way.

'Now remember,' he said emphatically, 'keep away from Flash Harry and his mob. The last man who informed on them ended up in the River Thames with a lead weight tied to his feet.'

CHAPTER 6

SUSPECTS

Alfie had the sausages fried and the beer cooling beside the draughty window of the cellar by the time his gang arrived home.

'Eat first and talk afterwards,' said Alfie. He knew by their faces that there was nothing much to report. He carefully poured the beer into the old pewter mugs while the sausages kept warm on the stone slab beside the fire. Alfie always insisted that everyone drank beer. His mother had died from cholera and a doctor had told him that she had got it from the water in the local pump. 'Drink beer, lad,' he had said to Alfie. 'People who drink nothing but beer don't get cholera.'

'Haven't got anything for you, Alfie,' said Sarah, spearing a sausage from the pan and popping it into her mouth. 'I got down to Trafalgar Square without anyone following me, but when I reached the statue of King Charles there were two men there and they were sweeping around it and levering up a manhole cover. I thought they might be workers, but then I saw that one had a pistol bulging in his back pocket so I took myself off.'

'You did the right thing,' said Alfie. 'I'll go down there later on myself. I'll wait until it gets dark. By then they'll either have found it or they'll have given up.' He felt quite cheerful as he chewed on his sausages and handed Jack his beer. 'Inspector Denham wants us to solve Jemmy's murder,' he said casually to his cousin. 'He thinks it might hold the key to the post office raid.'

Jack's face lit up. 'That's good,' he said, gulping down his beer and shooting a sausage in to follow it down his throat. 'Poor old Jemmy! If he has a funeral, I'll go to it.'

'I won't,' said Alfie with a shudder. 'Don't like that burying ground. Jemmy's not worth it.'

'Mutsy liked him,' Jack reminded him, tossing half a sausage over to where Mutsy lay dozing by the fire. Mutsy swallowed it down and sat up, his brown eyes bright behind the heavy fringe of fur.

'Now then, Mutsy, my boy, just you listen to the

facts.' Alfie popped another piece of sausage into the dog's mouth and playfully held the shaggy locks on either side of Mutsy's face. He tried to imitate Inspector Denham's dry voice. 'Pay attention now, young man, and never mind about sausages.'

'How many suspects?' asked Sammy.

'Well, that's the problem,' said Alfie. 'You see, he probably had lots of enemies. Like, when we was talking about it last night, I thought of Bert the Tosher, because Jack and me saw them have a terrible fight over a piece of gold.'

'And then there's Opium Sal,' said Sarah. 'You said he lodged free with her.'

'He told Jack that, didn't he, Jack?' Alfie looked over at his cousin.

'That's right. I asked him did he have to pay much and he just laughed. He said that she didn't have the nerve to ask him for a penny.'

'She asks for her money from those coves that take her drugs,' said Alfie. 'If she didn't ask Jemmy to pay for his lodging, she must have been scared of him for some reason.'

'And there's the fellow that I heard quarrelling with Jemmy last night. And Jemmy threatened to murder him,' said Jack.

'Three suspects,' said Sammy with satisfaction. 'I like

three. Not too many and not too few.'

'It might just be two,' put in Sarah, helping herself to another sausage. 'Jemmy was a big man. Opium Sal is a little woman and she's got the shakes as often as not. She could never have struck him on the forehead so hard that she killed him. But she might have hired someone to murder him. That might be the man that Jack heard quarrelling with Jemmy.'

'Might be,' said Jack dubiously. 'He didn't sound like he was from around here.'

'I like the idea of Opium Sal,' said Alfie slowly. He was thinking hard. 'You see, we need to find some sort of link between Jemmy and Flash Harry's mob, or else a link between him and some toff high up in the post office or one of them jewellers.'

'I don't think Jemmy would have anything to do with a toff,' said Jack doubtfully. 'He were a pretty rough sort of cove.'

'What do you think, Mutsy?' demanded Tom. 'One bark for a toff and two barks for Flash Harry's mob. Speak, Mutsy, speak!'

Mutsy gave one short bark and everyone laughed. And then there was a gasp from Sarah.

'The window!' she exclaimed. 'There's a face at the window!'

Alfie's head shot up and he saw something move over Jack's shoulder.

Sarah was right. There was a face there, someone on the pavement, bending down and looking in on them all, a face that was perfectly round, quite yellow in colour, with eyes that were large and vacant, dotted with tiny black pupils.

It was Opium Sal.

CHAPTER 7

THE NOTE

In a flash, Alfie was at the door and climbing up the steps of the cellar. By the time Sarah came out, he was standing on the pavement by the railings that fenced in the small deep-down yard in front of the cellar window.

'She got into a cab,' he said when Sarah and Jack joined him. 'Look, she's down there. Wonder what she wanted. Never saw her in a cab before. All her cash goes on buying opium.'

'Someone might have given her money to spy on you, to see whether you were at home.' Sarah felt uneasy, but there was little she could do. Alfie would go his own way. 'I'd better go to work,' she said. 'I'll be late otherwise.'

'And I'm going down to Trafalgar Square now, while this fog lasts,' said Alfie resolutely. Was Opium Sal looking in to see whether he had that piece of paper with the drawing on it? he wondered. If so, it showed how important it was – and not just to Flash Harry's mob. He gave a quick look up at the darkening sky. 'Looks as though it might be wet and windy later on.' In his mind was the worry that the sheet of paper might be blown away or washed out of its hiding place and turned into a pulp – that's if it had not been discovered already.

'Be careful, Alfie, and take Mutsy,' said Sarah as she walked off up Bow Street.

Alfie said nothing, but he didn't think that was good advice. Mutsy would make him too noticeable. When she had gone, he sent the dog back into the cellar and gave a nod of farewell to his cousin.

'I'm going with you,' said Jack stubbornly. 'I'm in this as much as you are.'

'Come on, then,' said Alfie. 'We should be all right for the moment. That fog is still too thick to see much. Wonder what Opium Sal is doing, riding around in a cab like a lady.'

Whatever she was doing, there was no sign of her when they reached the market, so they went on, threading their way through the stalls, and then down

33

the narrow lanes until they came to Trafalgar Square.

The square seemed empty after all the excitement of the night before. Alfie skirted it, keeping close to the buildings for as long as he could and then crossing the road swiftly. Once he reached the deep shadow thrown by the huge mounted statue, he started to relax. There did not appear to be anyone around, and the thick fog gave him extra cover.

He stood for a few minutes in front of the marble carving where he had hidden the note and tried to look casual. A few horse-drawn carriages passed by and then a cab. Alfie could see Jack's pale face over by the fountain in the centre, looking all around for any sign of Flash Harry's mob. He seemed to be satisfied because a moment later he crossed the road and stood beside Alfie. Still keeping his back to the ornamental stonework, Alfie felt blindly along it, probing with his fingers.

And then he had it! The hiding place had been good. The paper was still there and it was only slightly damp. It would still be readable, he hoped. He did not dare look at it, but concealed it inside his shirt.

And then he saw the man. He was wearing black clothes and had climbed on to the base of the statue, concealing himself behind the magnificent tail of the great black marble horse.

Alfie acted immediately. Touching Jack on the arm, he shot across the road towards the fountains and then bent down so that his head was below the high wall of the fountain basin. He had instantly seen that he had little chance of keeping out of pistol range if he crossed the empty space towards St Martin's Lane.

At that moment, the fog suddenly cleared. Purple clouds were shot with a streak of lightning, then there was a rumble of thunder and the rain began, great slanting sheets of it sweeping down on the dirty pavements.

'Keep down!' Alfie hissed to Jack, who was close behind him. 'Follow me.' He was glad that he had not brought Mutsy. The dog was as brave as a lion, but no living thing stood a chance against a gun.

Keeping their heads well down, Alfie and Jack scuttled along until they were opposite some large trees. There was no gas lamp near to them, so Alfie took a chance. With a hasty glance over his shoulder, he bolted across. In a moment, he and Jack were behind the blackened tree trunks.

The man had moved out of the shadow of Nelson's Column and was making his way, slowly and deliberately, towards the basin where the water splashed down from the fountain above. He had a hand thrust into a pocket and it was easy to imagine a pistol clasped within.

Alfie held his breath. He peered out from behind the trees, waiting until the man was facing the National Gallery with his back towards Nelson's Column. Then he and Jack exploded, running as fast as they could towards Cockspur Street.

Two minutes to go up Cockspur and into Haymarket, another minute to reach the White Horse, his thoughts raced along as he ran. Jack was beside him now. Sarah would be at work in the White Horse Inn by this time. If they could only get there, she might be able to hide them for a few hours.

Once they reached the broad street of Haymarket he glanced over his shoulder. There was no sign of any pursuer but one could appear at any moment.

Alfie stopped and drew Jack into the shadow of the wall. They could slink along here unseen. He prayed that the man had not seen their frantic bolt for Cockspur Street – hopefully, he would be looking for them in St Martin's Lane. If he was in the same mob as the man who followed them home earlier, then he knew where the boys lived.

But no! A figure dressed in black suddenly appeared, so brightly lit by the gas lamp at the bottom of Haymarket that they could see a small red scarf knotted around his throat. He was talking to a second man who had come down Haymarket, who now turned around and pointed. The man with the red scarf nodded.

At that moment, a large brewery wagon, drawn by six heavy horses, came slowly up Haymarket. It ground along laboriously, the big wooden beer barrels creaking and the wheels rumbling. In an instant, Alfie darted out and scrambled on board, crouching down behind one of the barrels. A second later, Jack joined him, hiding behind another barrel.

The wagon moved slowly but Alfie did not care. Flash Harry's mob had a reputation for being smooth operators, smooth and careful. They would not take any risk while the brewery men were around. As soon as the brewery van took the expected turn into the yard of the White Horse Inn, Alfie stuck a cautious head out from behind the barrel. They had gone through the gate and were now turning again to go into the back yard. Once they were out of sight of the road, Alfie jumped down, closely followed by Jack.

By the time the two brewery men came around to the back of the wagon, the two boys were just standing there, looking as if they had come in from the street, one politely doffing his cap and saying, 'Give you a hand with the barrels, mister?'

'Just a couple of pennies, and you'll have to share them between you,' warned the driver.

Alfie nodded gratefully. He would have helped them for nothing. While he and Jack were in their company they were safe. Everyone knew that brewery workers were tough. They were always huge men with muscles that stood out like knotted cords on their arms and they were used to battling their way through the crowded streets of London where their enormous wagons were most unpopular. Flash Harry's mobsters would not meddle with them even if they did follow the boys into the yard.

'Roll it over there,' grunted the driver's mate, landing a barrel at Jack's feet. Jack had done this sort of work before and neatly spun the barrel across the yard towards the hatch where the innkeeper's head appeared. Alfie followed and a working rhythm was set up. It was hard work, especially in the driving rain, but it took Alfie's mind off the danger and after a while he began to enjoy himself. In the beginning the innkeeper had to wait for them, but after ten minutes it was the other way around.

'Well done, lads, here's a thruppenny piece for you,' said the driver when all the barrels had been stored in the cellar.

'And here's another to bring it up to sixpence,' said the innkeeper.

'All right if we get a drink of water in the scullery?' asked Alfie casually. He had been racking his brains as to how he could get in touch with Sarah. Her job was serving meals and drinks in the parlour of the White Horse. Would she be finished work yet? he wondered.

'That's all right, and ask the scullery maid if there's a bit of broken pie left over,' said the innkeeper generously. 'We're that busy,' he continued, gossiping to the brewery men, 'we've a crowd of engineers from Birmingham staying here and they like to walk around London at night, and then come back and eat and drink the rest of the night away! I'm glad to get this delivery tonight. I'd begun to think they would drink the house dry!' He laughed heartily and the brewery men joined in.

Alfie nodded to Jack and they both crossed the paved yard silently on their bare feet and opened the scullery door. Alfie stopped to peer in the window. Kitty the scullery maid was in there – that was all right, they had met her a few times when they came to see Sarah. She was bad-temperedly scrubbing a burned pan with a handful of sand and scowled as they entered.

'If you're looking for Sarah,' she said, 'she's working. That crowd from Birmingham have started eating and drinking in the blue parlour.'

'Just came to give you a hand,' said Alfie promptly, seizing the saucepan and the scrubbing brush and setting to work vigorously. He put all his strength into the work and soon the pot was looking pretty good, but he tackled it again just to show how hard-working he was and spent another few minutes on it. Jack made himself useful at the sink, washing a pile of dirty dishes. The two boys started with alarm as they heard heavy footsteps on the stairs outside.

'That's just Matt, the boot boy,' said Kitty. 'You in trouble, you two?'

'Nah,' said Alfie nonchalantly, but he was tense until the door opened and showed the fat face of the boot boy.

'I'm going to be up all night,' said Matt, coming in and slumping on a stool. 'That lot from Birmingham don't know when to go to bed. It's going to be the same as last night. They'll go to bed at two or three o'clock in the morning and then expect their boots to be waiting outside their door, all clean and shiny, by eight o'clock next morning.'

'Oh, stop moaning,' said Kitty. 'All you have to do is polish the boots and clean the knives. You should try my job. Anyway, there's a pair of boots over there to keep you busy while you're waiting for them to go to bed. They belong to the gentleman from Birmingham that's sick in bed in number fifteen. Sarah said you were to clean them again. She said they're still a disgrace.'

'She should have seen them the first time,' grumbled Matt. 'When that geezer came home last night the leather was soaked through and they smelt like a drain – don't know what he trod in.'

'Boss said you'd give us a drink and a piece of broken pie; we've been helping him with the barrels,' said Alfie, still scrubbing vigorously.

'You can have that saucepan of milk if you like,' said Kitty, pointing. 'The sick gent fancied some boiled milk but it over-boiled. Smells dreadful!'

'Tastes all right,' said Alfie, gulping some down. He passed the half-full saucepan of milk on to Jack and looked around at the dirty plates for some pieces of pie. Amazing what folks left on their plates, he thought, as he and Jack wolfed down the tasty fragments.

'There's Sarah coming down now,' said Kitty. 'I know her step. She's lighter than the other parlour maid.'

Sarah was quick and clever, though, and Alfie thought highly of her brains. He wished that he could show her the note, safely stored inside his shirt, but her first words turned his mind in a different direction.

'Alfie,' she hissed. 'What are you doing here? Get away quickly! There's a man in the bar looking for two ragged boys. He's dressed in black, wearing a red scarf. Do you know him? I heard the landlord tell him that he had just sent two boys of that description down to the kitchen. The man's on his way now!'

41

CHAPTER 8

UNDERGROUND

Almost before the words had left Sarah's mouth, Alfie was through the door like a streak of lightning. Behind him, he heard Jack close the door quietly and then run after him, his bare feet slapping the rough cobbles of the yard.

But they could not escape. Standing at the gate, looking out on to the street, was another man, a mob member no doubt, and he had his right hand in his pocket. No, he and Jack must hide until the men had gone and Alfie knew just the place to do so. They had lowered enough beer barrels down from the yard during the last half-hour.

Made desperate by fear, Alfie managed to lever up the iron cover to the cellar, leaving his fingerails broken and bleeding.

The chute where the barrels had rolled only twenty minutes ago was still in place. Alfie curled himself into a ball, head tucked under his arms, feet drawn up to his chest, and rolled rapidly down. As he landed on the bristly mat, he looked back and saw Jack at the top of the chute, carefully edging the manhole cover back into place above him. It seemed to take an agonisingly long time, but eventually it was closed and the cellar was thrown into total darkness. Alfie held his breath, listening to the sounds of Jack fumbling his way down the chute.

At first he could see nothing and he took tiny steps forward, feeling the space in front of him with his hands. It would never do to blunder into a barrel and knock it over. Thick cords of spiders' webs clung to his face and his hands. He held his breath to avoid filling his lungs with the dust clouds that clotted his mouth and nostrils.

Then Jack sneezed vigorously and Alfie's heart nearly stopped. Nothing happened, so after a minute he went on moving, his bare feet feeling the rough wooden floor beneath, listening so intently that his head hurt with the strain of it.

However, there was no sound from behind them or

the yard. No shouting, no rattling of the metal chute cover. He hoped that the man with the pistol would think that they had gone back out on to Haymarket.

So far all was going well. Alfie took no chances, though. Someone might just have the brains to think of the cellar. Giving Jack's sleeve a quick jerk, he edged his way across towards what he hoped was the centre of the cellar, planning to find a hiding place among the beer barrels that were stored there, well away from the damp cellar walls.

Suddenly Jack touched Alfie on the shoulder and spoke directly into his ear. 'There's the door up to the bar.'

Alfie turned back and saw a line of light dimly illuminating a rectangular door shape and a keyhole. He stopped. Now they were halfway between the door and the chute. If anyone came in from either of these two entrances, at least they might be able to escape through the other.

There was a sudden scuffle in front of them. Both boys jumped in alarm – there must be rats around. Alfie shuddered, wishing that he had Mutsy with him – he hated rats as much as Mutsy loved them. If we get out of this alive, thought Alfie, I'll take him to Covent Garden market – plenty of rats there. Smiling at the thought, he settled down with his back to a barrel, and Jack did the same.

From upstairs came roars and guffaws of laughter and the raucous sound of drunken men singing 'Pop goes the Weasel'. Someone was banging on the bar shouting, 'We want beer! We want beer!' Someone else was yelling, 'Ned, Ned, where are you? C'mon, what's got into you, Ned? Never knew you to be so unsociable!'

After a while, Alfie ceased to listen and drifted off into a deep sleep. From time to time he stirred sleepily, but Jack, by the sound of his breathing, was also sleeping, so he settled back again, and only woke when a tinge of dawn light came through the small window of the cellar.

Jack was already awake and was standing up, his head on one side. 'Alfie, do you hear something?' he whispered.

Alfie listened. For a moment, all he heard were a few cries of seagulls out in the yard. In the dimness, he saw his cousin kneel down and put the side of his face against the floor.

'There, hear that,' he said.

Alfie crouched and lowered one ear towards the floor. 'There's something under there,' he breathed as quietly as he could, 'something's moving under there just below us.'

'Listen again,' whispered Jack.

He didn't sound worried, so Alfie took in a deep breath. For a moment he had thought it might be a swarm of rats moving along beneath them, but now he realised that it was something else. 'There's water down there,' he said.

'That's what I reckon.'

'What is it? Where does the water come from?' whispered Alfie.

'Could be one of them underground rivers – there's rivers all over London, someone told me. London used to be once just fields with rivers running through them and then the houses came and there were so many houses they started to build roads over the rivers and then they took to building houses over the roads and making new roads. That's what I heard, anyways.' Jack's voice was as placid as ever and did not change when he added, 'And, of course, people empty their drains and their cesspits into these underground rivers. That's why London is such a smelly place and why it has so many rats.'

Alfie felt the floor of the cellar, shuddering. It was made of wooden planks. Not good, he thought, remembering the woman in the privy in one of those crazy, half fallen-down houses in the slums of St Giles. She had fallen through the rotten floorboards and had drowned in the cesspool beneath. And her child had gone with her.

'Who told you all that stuff?' Alfie hoped that his voice did not betray how nervous he was. He wished he was out of that dark cellar which smelt of mould. 'Bert the Tosher, was it?' he added.

'No, it were old Jemmy that told me about the underground rivers. He knew a lot, did Jemmy. He used to work in the sewers when he was a bit younger, but then he gave it up after he had the cholera. He said that when he was sick he swore if ever he recovered he would never go down a sewer again. Dead now, poor old fellow, and not from the sewers neither,' Jack sighed.

'Wouldn't like going down there myself,' said Alfie with a shudder. 'Too many rats down there for me! They say that some of them are as big as cats and as fierce as bulls.'

'There's a manhole cover, here.' Jack's hand was feeling around.

'Leading down to the river?'

'That's right. The drains from the cesspits lead down into it. Places like inns often just put their rubbish straight down into sewers.'

'Good,' said Alfie, trying hard not to think about rats. 'Perhaps we could drop down there and go along it like the toshers do. Let's lever it up now and be ready to disappear down if anyone comes.'

'Shh!' said Jack warningly.

Alfie gulped.

Beyond the gleam of light from the cellar window came the sound of heavy footsteps, the scrape of a key in the lock and then the creak of a door handle. Alfie froze, his shoulder touching Jack's, ready to spring.

CHAPTER 9

BLOOD MONEY

One of the things that Sarah liked best about her new job as parlour maid at the White Horse Inn was that, as soon as the breakfasts had been served, she could leave the inn until the time for the next meal came up.

And so it was that she was strolling up Bow Street at ten o'clock in the morning. It was a nice day, she thought. After the storm of last night, the air seemed fresher and cleaner than usual in London, as though the city had been thoroughly washed by the heavy rain which had not ceased until about one o'clock in the morning.

'I'll go and check whether the boys are all right,' she said to herself. There had been no sign of Alfie or Jack after she had brought the warning to them. They had disappeared with the speed of lightning.

But there was no one at home in the cellar on Bow Street, not even Mutsy. She knocked again loudly, just to make sure, but there was no bark of greeting, or sound of a large nose sniffing at the door. Sarah clicked her tongue with annoyance. She was the sort of person who always liked to know whether things were going well, or whether a problem had arisen. Problems she could deal with, but uncertainty was more difficult. She knocked again just to be absolutely sure and softly called 'Mutsy', but no, he was definitely not there.

At this hour of the morning, Alfie and the rest of the gang would usually have gone out, but Jack, who worked by night, would normally still be sleeping – and last night, Alfie had also been out late. Either they had already gone out, or else Alfie and Jack had not returned the night before.

Sarah shivered slightly as she remembered the hard, dangerous eyes of the man who had been looking for two lads at the inn. Had he found them after all? He and his friend had not returned to the White Horse with the Birmingham engineers who had accompanied him on the chase.

'Seen Alfie, anywhere?' she asked the butcher who

was standing in front of his window, supervising a boy who was sweeping out the sodden piles of wood shavings and flood water from his shop.

'Haven't seen him this morning. Saw the blind boy, though. And the other young lad, and the big dog. Dragging some sort of board with him, he was.' The butcher spoke impatiently over his shoulder. He wasn't interested. He was trying to get his shop in order before the customers came.

Sarah was mystified. What was Tom doing with a board? She puzzled over it for a moment, trying to distract herself from the cold fear in the back of her mind that the man with the scarf had captured Alfie and Jack.

'Perhaps I'll go over to Trafalgar Square,' she muttered to herself. The chances were that Tom and Sammy would be over there, Sammy singing on the steps of St Martin-in-the-Fields church and Tom searching the fountain for coins that people often threw in there for luck.

The poster was still outside the police station when she came up to it and people were still gossiping about the daring raid on the post office.

'I heard that fifty gold bars were stolen,' said a baker, balancing his basket with one arm and staring at the poster.

'I heard that it were jewels,' said a bare-footed boy.

'They've never had such a thing happen at that post

office before,' said the woman beside Sarah. Her voice was loud and excited and several people stopped to listen. 'My husband was there. They were just loading up the mailbags when someone shouted out, *Fire!* and the place was full of smoke. Of course they all rushed outside. The fire turned out to be in the coffee room at Morley's Hotel and they were all standing there looking up when the mail van drove out.'

'Didn't they see the robbers go in, then?' asked a stout lady with a shopping basket.

'Sneaked in by the side entrance didn't they?' retorted the wife of the post office worker. She sounded quite annoyed, as though her husband was accused of not doing his duty. 'Nobody expected it. Bold as brass, they were. Picked up all the mailbags and drove out and were gone before anyone thought to question them.'

'Well, they'll be hanged when they're caught, that's certain,' said the stout lady.

'*If* they're caught,' said a man. He had been standing on the other side of the road, but came across to join the little crowd around the police station. He looked as if he might be a street beggar, with torn, ragged clothes and eyes bright with starvation or fever. 'Not sure that I'd like to turn in any of that mob – they say Flash Harry never forgives and never forgets.' He looked around and then gave a quick shudder and shuffled away as rapidly as he could.

Sarah looked over her shoulder, following the direction of his eyes as he had looked down the street. There, just opposite the cellar where the boys lived, a man was standing.

And he was wearing a red scarf.

Sarah stared fearfully at the man for a few minutes. Surely that was the man who had come into the bar last night looking for the boys? He was leaning against the wall of a shop, picking his teeth idly with a straw. She noticed that his eyes only moved from the cellar steps to give a quick hasty glance down Bow Street, and then came back again to focus on the cellar where the four boys lived. He looked as though he were prepared to wait patiently there all day until his victim turned up.

There was something odd about the way that the man stood there, something rigid about him. His left hand held the straw, but his right hand was stuck deep into his pocket. Sarah narrowed her eyes and drew in a sharp breath as she saw the shape of a gun outlined within the pocket.

Casually, Sarah crossed the road, taking care not to allow her eyes to meet those of the watcher. He was definitely the same man. He must have seen her last night, but she had been in the background, loading her tray with drinks for the parlour where the engineers from Birmingham clamoured for more beer. It was unlikely that he would have bothered looking at a parlour maid. She was safe for the moment.

And then something odd happened. Opium Sal came shuffling along Bow Street. That was the second time she had been seen there. Why would she bother to climb the steep hill from her home on Hungerford Lane? She, too, seemed to be interested in the cellar where the boys lived.

She limped along the pavement towards it, muttering to herself, and then, suddenly, she stopped. Her eyes met those of the watcher across the road. Sarah held her breath. Were they in league?

No – the watching man took no notice of the old lady. No sign or look of recognition came from him. But Opium Sal seemed to recognise him. She turned on her heel and went straight back in the direction from which she had come.

Sarah wondered whether to follow her to see where she went. However, she could not just walk away and leave the boys at the mercy of the armed watcher. She had to do something.

Sarah walked quickly until she reached Bow Street police station. Once inside, she went straight up to the tall wooden counter where a policeman was writing busily in a notebook.

'I'd like to see Inspector Denham,' she said in a firm voice. 'I have some information for him from Alfie Sykes. It concerns the post office raid.'

CHAPTER 10

DROWNED RATS

The stench made Alfie gasp for a moment, but the noise of the cellar bolt creaking was enough to make him drop immediately down into the water that rushed along at the bottom of the underground passage. He landed on his feet, skidded and then fell into the water, just managing to keep his face out of the slime and filth that floated along on its surface. His hand grabbed a protruding piece of brick and, as he hauled himself back to his feet, Alfie saw a rat running up the steeply curved wall of the tunnel.

Jack managed better, grabbing an iron ring set into the brickwork of the tunnel and lowering himself cautiously down once he had pulled the cover into position again.

Alfie drew in a deep breath. So this was the sewer below the cellar of the White Horse Inn. Further down the tunnel a faint glow was coming from somewhere. He stood for a minute, allowing his eyes time to become accustomed to the dimness, and then he began to move cautiously down the sewer. He could hear Jack splashing behind him, but he kept going steadily, trying to hold his breath as long as he could. The stench was more horrible than anything he met in his daily life – worse even than the stink around Smithfield market. But after a few minutes he no longer noticed and began to breathe normally, concentrating on the dim light ahead of them.

'Pitch torches,' said Jack from behind him. His voice echoed weirdly, bouncing off the brick walls of the tunnel and coming back to them as if ten boys had spoken.

'How do you know?' Alfie tried to whisper, but the hissing echo was even more sinister.

'Bert the Tosher told me. Remember that time I dragged Jemmy off him? When he met me later on he thanked me. He offered me a job working with him and his family. He told me a lot about working down here. Said that it wasn't as bad as people thought.'

'I remember.' Alfie nodded. He wouldn't forget easily that spectacular fight down by the river a few weeks ago.

Jack and he had been gathering pieces of coal from the

shallow waters of the river and had moved downstream towards Whitehall, as there was not much left around the Hungerford Stairs where so many poor people scavenged a living. They were nearly there when Bert the Tosher emerged from the Tyburn sewer.

Bert had washed his face and hands in the river water, dabbing with his sleeve at a large cut on his forehead. Then he had taken something from his pocket and cleaned it carefully. Alfie and Jack had been near enough to see a flash of gold and had looked at each other, wide-eyed. It was known that men like Bert did the dangerous and dirty work of keeping the sewers flowing, not just for the low wages they got, but for the occasional finds – a gold watch or maybe some jewellery – that were washed down from the privies or carried off with the sink water from the old inns of London.

But gold! Here was a find! Two large squares of gold, each the size of a sovereign and held together with a gold bar. Bert had been gazing at it lovingly when Jemmy had erupted from the tunnel, brandishing one of those heavy sticks that toshers carried to drive the rats away from around their feet. In a moment, he was on top of Bert, knocking him to the ground and beating him unmercifully with the stick.

Alfie had winced at the sound of the blows; each one

of them was enough to break the man's skull. Jack, however, did not hesitate. He launched himself at the tangled figures on the water's edge and hung onto Jemmy's arm with all his might, twisting it upwards while Alfie snatched the stick and flung it far out into the river. And then both of them had moved away quickly just in case Jemmy turned on them. But he didn't . . .

'Funny, wasn't it, how they lost the gold thing in the mud and then the two of them immediately began searching the mud together like they was the best of friends?' Alfie grinned at the memory.

'Not such great friends,' said Jack, sloshing through the water behind him, his voice bouncing from wall to wall, every word repeated endlessly, so that they jumbled into each other. 'The next time that I met Bert, he told me that he was going to kill Jemmy for losing that thing – a gold cufflink, it was, like posh men wear in their sleeves. Bert found it in the sewer under Buckingham Palace where Queen Victoria lives and then Jemmy half-murdered him, and the cufflink was gone for good. No wonder Bert bore him a grudge. That gold cufflink would have been worth a lot to Bert – what with all his children and everything. I wonder if he had anything to do with old Jemmy's murder . . .' Jack stopped.

Alfie looked over his shoulder to see his cousin

standing very still, looking all around him.

'What's up?' asked Alfie. He was getting used to the echo now and not finding the passageway through the sewers too bad. If the toshers did it every day for a living, surely he and Jack could survive the experience once. Already he was planning how they would clean themselves under the pump at Whitehall, if that was where they emerged.

'Seems wrong somehow.' Jack's voice sounded uneasy. 'It's been pouring rain, could hear it bouncing off the cobbles in the yard all night. But look at the water! It's hardly moving.'

'What's wrong with that?' asked Alfie impatiently.

'Too low.' Jack looked up and down, surveying the green waters and their slow-moving sludge. 'Bert told me that they have to open gates when there's heavy rain,' he added. 'Seems like they might have forgot to do that upstream. Hampstead ponds will all be overflowing and pouring down into the drains. There'll be a gate between here and Hampstead that someone has forgotten to open.'

'So —' began Alfie.

The word was hardly out of his lips when there was a strange sound. It boomed like thunder. It roared like the wild beasts in Astley's Circus. It bounced off the arched roof. Alfie felt as though his eardrums would burst. He looked over his shoulder.

And there, in an ear-splitting explosion of sound, an enormous wall of water as high as the ceiling came thundering down towards them.

'Run!' screamed Jack.

Alfie ran, stumbling through the sludgy water. He did not need to look over his shoulder to know that he had no hope of escaping the wall of water that roared its way down through the tunnel. Jack was beside him now, holding his arm. That was the way they would find the bodies, thought Alfie. Two cousins, one's hand locked in a grip on the arm of the other.

The water was chest-high now. Something thudded against his back and then swept past him. It was a family of drowned rats – ten, twenty, even forty of them. Alfie did not even shudder, seeing his own fate mirrored in these soaked dead bodies, swirling on the foaming water.

This deadly flood would sweep them along the sewer and spit them out into the River Thames at Whitehall.

And by then they would both be dead.

CHAPTER 11

BLOCKED

One minute it seemed as though they might have a chance – if only they had superhuman legs that could stride through the water at the speed of lightning. But the next minute it was all over.

Alfie had never felt such power in his life. Effortlessly, the roaring water snatched him from Jack's grasp and he was swept on, turning and twisting as though his body was the size of a rat's. The flood was almost ceiling high, now; Alfie felt his head crash against the rough old bricks. He panted like a man running for his life. The water seemed to have taken all the air out of the sewer. Jack passed him, his body spinning around in the water.

Alfie followed it with his eyes. This would be his last sight of his cousin, he thought. Even someone as brave and resourceful as Jack could do nothing in a flood like this.

Suddenly Jack's body stopped. Alfie crashed into him and felt a hand grip his coat. He blinked the water from his eyes. Jack had caught hold of one of those iron rings set firmly into the ceiling. Alfie felt around and inserted his own cold hand beside Jack's. He hung on desperately as the water tugged at the rags of his clothing, dragged his legs, made him feel as though he would snap in two at any minute. How long could they manage to hold on? Even after a minute, he felt as though his body was being ripped in two.

And then Alfie realised something else. The heavy iron ring was no longer holding him steadily. It had begun to loosen. One side of it was ripped from the ceiling. The screw had given way. Alfie felt bits of broken brick fall on his forehead before they, too, were swept away. Every muscle in his body ached with the strain of holding himself taut against the pull of the flood.

Now it was only a matter of time before the second screw was gone. One part of Alfie almost wished that it was all over, but the other part – the tough part – was scanning the arched ceiling for something else, anything else, to hang on to. This flood had to go down some time. Surely someone would open a gate further down and allow the water to escape into the river.

And then the second screw parted from the ceiling. Alfie let go of the useless circle of metal and allowed it drop down through the water. For a moment, he caught a glimpse of Jack just ahead of him. His cousin was being swept helplessly on the flood. Then he was gone and Alfie followed him, shooting forwards, his eyes on the brick ceiling above him as he strove to keep his mouth clear.

Suddenly, the ceiling wasn't there. A large egg-like space rose up above them. As he shot past he could see that this raised section was where the pitch torches flared in their iron sockets, lighting up the water below. The air was better here and Alfie managed to draw in a lungful before he was swept on. The sight of that tall arched area gave him a moment's hope. Perhaps they were nearing the end of the sewer, were near to the place where it poured out on the bank at Whitehall, where he and Jack had witnessed the fight between old Jemmy and Bert the Tosher.

But there was no light ahead of them now, just an inky blackness. He could no longer see Jack – and that was the worst moment. Had Jack drowned? And how much longer could he survive himself?

This is it, he concluded, and he spared a thought for Sammy. How would the blind boy manage without his brother to look after him?

And then, above the noise of the flood, he thought he heard something. He tried to get his head free of the water. Yes, there it was again – a long wail.

'A – l – f – i – e!'

But the warning came too late.

Alfie felt the blow before he saw anything.

The crash almost knocked him unconscious, but then he rallied. He had come to a full stop against a great barrier made from wooden slabs. One of them was broken – a piece the length of his arm was missing – which was enough for Alfie to stick his hand through and grab on to the barrier; enough to stop him being swept under the water.

The water flowed through the gaps between the slabs, but it was still violent and Alfie felt blow after blow pummel his body until he thought that he could not bear it any longer.

However, a faint gleam of light came through the broken slab and soon his eyes became used to the darkness and he was able to see a little. This was one of the storm gates, he realised: great squared-off chunks of wood, piled almost to the height of the ceiling.

'Alfie!' the shout came again and this time he located it, looking upwards. Jack was on top of the storm gate, clinging on. He was pointing to the side of the gate, and it took Alfie a few moments to make out rusty chains hanging down. The gate must be raised and lowered with these chains. Alfie was reluctant to let go of his safe hold on the broken plank, but what Jack had done, he could do. Clenching his teeth and keeping his courage up with thoughts of Sammy and Mutsy waiting for him, he launched himself into the seething water, kicking his legs frantically and clawing with his arms.

The relief when his outstretched hand clenched the chain was so enormous that for a moment he just hung on, too weak to move. But then he began to climb rapidly and was soon on top of the storm gate at Jack's side.

Jack said nothing but began to climb the chain again, hand over hand, bare toes gripping the large loops. Now they were both well above the gate and scaling a stone wall. Here and there, more iron circles were set solidly into the wall and they used these as footholds as they swarmed up the rusty chain.

'There'll be a manhole, a hatch at the top of this,' grunted Jack after a few minutes. 'Somebody should be thinking of opening this gate soon, but with some luck we'll get out first.'

Alfie did not answer. He needed all of his energy for the climb. Every bone in his body ached after the pummelling of the flood water. He had an awful fear in his mind that from sheer exhaustion and weakness the chain would slip from between his fingers and he would crash down into that terrible sewer again.

I'll count to ten and then look up, he told himself. And then another ten, and then another ten.

And when the thirty was counted out, Alfie saw to his surprise that he was almost at the top.

'Let's get out of here as quick as we can,' he said when he joined Jack at the little platform beside the hatch.

And together they pushed up the metal slab.

Alfie's hand went to his shirt. He had carefully concealed the note dropped by Flash Harry there.

But all that remained was a sodden lump of pulp.

CHAPTER 12

SAMMY ALONE

Sammy missed Mutsy. Tom had grudgingly escorted him to the corner of Covent Garden but then had left him, taking Mutsy with him and muttering something about how hungry he was. Sammy was too worried about Alfie and Jack to feel hunger, but he understood how badly Tom wanted to earn some money for his breakfast.

'It's just such a good morning for Jack's board on wheels,' Tom had explained to him before they set out. 'It's been pouring all night. I bet the crossing at Piccadilly Circus is flooded. Jack and me have been practising. We put Mutsy on the board and I tow him across the road and this gets everyone looking – brings a crowd. Next I ask if anyone wants to cross the road without getting their feet wet. I help a lady to stand on the board and hold onto the handle in front and then I pull her across the street and let her step, nice and dry, onto the pavement on the other side. We've been waiting for a good, wet day to try it out and I don't want to waste these floods. You'll be all right on your own, won't you, Sammy? I'll come and pick you up when I'm finished – if you're not there, I'll look for you by St Martin's church. You're sure to find someone to take you there.'

Sammy would have preferred to go with Tom and Mutsy, but he realised that Tom did not want him distracting attention from his wheeled plank. However, he did not want to stay in the cellar alone so he nodded silently and allowed Tom to leave him beside the apple seller in Covent Garden market. He did his best to sing, but there was no thud of coins falling into the cap he had placed on the ground in front of him. His voice was high, pure and sweet, but it wasn't a loud voice and Covent Garden was too noisy a place for his song to attract an audience. He needed someone to call attention to him, to walk up to people and ask them if they wanted to hear a song. Eventually Sammy fell silent and began to worry instead of sing.

It wasn't like Alfie to stay out all night, thought Sammy.

If only his brother hadn't had the notion to go to Trafalgar Square. It would have been better if they had had Mutsy with them. Mutsy was a good guard and if anything had happened to Alfie and Jack, the dog would have saved them or come back to the cellar. Sammy's mind turned to the time when he himself had been almost drowned and Mutsy, the hero, had brought Alfie to rescue him.

When he'd heard the church bells strike midnight last night, he had persuaded Tom to take the dog to Trafalgar Square, but Tom had returned with no news of the boys. Where were Alfie and Jack? Sammy had stayed awake for a long time, but eventually he had fallen asleep.

And when he woke the two older boys were still missing . . .

'All right, sonny?' Sammy's thoughts were interrupted by a quavering voice, the words followed by a series of loud hiccups. Sammy smiled. He knew who this was. Mick had been a friend of his grandfather's. *Drinks like a fish*, his grandfather used to say, *but a heart of gold*, he always added.

'Look at the lovely smile on him!' exclaimed Mick. He was drunk, but not too drunk, decided Sammy.

'I'm having no luck this morning, Mick,' he said. 'Would you be able to take me over to Trafalgar Square? I do better there, usually.'

'Anything in the world that you want, just ask Mick MacClancy!' The words were slurred but they were accompanied by a warm hug of Sammy's shoulders. 'And I'll stay with you too,' went on Mick. 'I'll have a bit of a snooze if I can and you wake me up when you want to go home. There's some sun for a change and it will do my old bones a lot of good. That's the trouble with me, Sammy, my bones. If it wasn't for my bones I'd never touch a drop of drink.'

Sammy nodded, holding back a smile, and groped with his hand to attach himself to Mick's sleeve. If he did well at St Martin's church he would give the old man the price of a drink, he decided. He turned his face upwards, thinking that the sun wouldn't last too long. There was a stillness and a moistness in the air that told him the fog would soon return, but he said nothing to Mick as they trudged through the crowded wet streets, just listened smilingly to the chatter about the old days in Ireland and the markets where the boys' grandfather had played his fiddle.

'Hey, you! You with the blinkers!' The man's voice was sharp and Mick came to an abrupt halt.

Sammy turned his face towards the speaker. 'Blinkers' was a slang term for blind eyes and he was used to boys shouting it at him. Not adults though, usually, and this voice sounded aggressive. Beneath his fingers he felt Mick's arm tense. He hoped that the old man would not suddenly depart, leaving him alone with this harsh-voiced man.

'Live in a cellar in Bow Street – that's right, ain't it?'

'That's right.' Sammy kept his voice steady. Mick shuffled his feet uneasily.

'Got a couple of brothers. Two lads with dark hair?'

Sammy nodded again. There was a certain sound from this man's voice, a sound that only someone with Sammy's gifts could interpret. Just as a sighted person could read faces and watch gestures, Sammy could pick up the stink of fear, anger, aggression and evil – what his grandfather called scenting the smell of wolf.

This man is ready to attack, he thought, and he exercised all his skill to make sure that no hesitation or worry sounded in his voice.

'They're gone into the country with one of them market gardeners,' he said carelessly. 'Got a few days' work picking Brussels sprouts for Covent Garden costermongers. Was you wanting them for a job? Be back early next week.'

'And who's looking after you then? You left on your own?' The man's voice was sharp with suspicion.

'Naw.' Sammy had a keen ear and knew that he

sounded unconcerned. 'Young Tom – he's the youngest of us – he's looking after me and Mick here.' He turned his blind eyes towards the old man.

There was a moment's silence. The man with the harsh voice would be looking at Sammy, staring at him, trying to make up his mind whether the boy was telling the truth. One of the advantages of being blind, thought Sammy with an inward chuckle, was that his face would be hard to read. He had often heard Alfie say to Tom, 'You'd better tell the truth! I can see it in your eyes when you don't.'

And then Sammy stiffened. By the sound of it, the man was fumbling in his pocket. Sammy could hear the sound, but also he could smell something. It was the same smell that you got from matches, but this was stronger. Sammy immediately knew what it was. He had passed that factory often and Alfie had explained to him about bullets and how they worked in guns. The man smelt of gunpowder.

And he probably had a loaded pistol in his pocket.

CHAPTER 13

DEMONS
FROM HELL

It was a long time since Sammy had yearned to be able to see like other people. His grandfather had gently talked him out of thinking like that and had diverted his attention to clever ways of knowing what was happening around him. Nevertheless, after his wakeful night of worrying about Alfie and Jack, Sammy felt unsure and useless.

If only he could *see* what Mick and the man with the pistol were doing! Would Mick betray him? Sadly, he felt that the old man was not to be trusted.

Sammy's mind went to Alfie. This man must be part of Flash Harry's mob. They'd cared enough about that bit of paper with the clock drawing to chase Alfie halfway across London. He'd given them the slip, but now they were hoping that Sammy would lead them to his brother. Sammy stood very still and said nothing and hoped that his face betrayed nothing.

For the moment there was silence and he was almost relieved when that silence was broken.

'Here you! Old man! Come over here. I want a word with you.' The voice of the man with the pistol was clipped and full of authority. Mick immediately pulled his arm away. Sammy stood very still and strained his ears, hearing Mick suck in his breath sharply. The two men had gone a little distance and their whispers were very low. Broken bits of sentences came to him. 'I have to get hold of that boy . . . I'll find you . . . I'll be keeping an eye on you . . .' And then the clink of money in the man's pocket and an exclamation of dismay from Mick.

'Not now,' said the man, a teasing note of amusement in his voice. 'I only pay when goods are delivered. That young Alfie is as slippery as an eel, but if you're right he'll come quick enough once he knows that I have his brother.'

There was a mutter from Mick and then the mobster broke in, anger making his voice louder than before, 'No, you old fool! If I drag that blind boy kicking and screaming through Covent Garden market, then half the stallholders will be after me. No, you go along with him to Trafalgar Square, let him sing his song and then bring him over to the archway. I'll be waiting for you there and I'll take him off your hands.'

Then he turned and Sammy heard his iron-tipped heels clanking down the street.

'Where are the other boys then, Sammy?' Mick's tone was almost casual as they made their way along through the crowds, but his voice shook and there was an underlying note of anxiety – and of guilt.

Mick, thought Sammy, would betray Alfie or himself for the price of a drink or two. He would not be able to help himself. *Never trust a man who drinks*, the boys' grandfather used to say. *You might think that he likes you, wouldn't let you down, but only drink really matters to him.*

'Well, Alfie and Jack went off on a job picking Brussels sprouts for the market gardener, like I said,' said Sammy, pleased to hear how innocent his voice sounded, 'and Tom has taken his board on wheels up to Piccadilly Circus.' Tom would be doing well, he thought, as he and Mick splashed through ankle-high water as they crossed a road. No lady would want to risk ruining her dress in water like that.

'This where you want to go? This is the church,' said Mick, coming to a halt.

It was cold here by St Martin's. There was no sun on the west-facing steps at this hour of the morning.

There were not many people around the church, either – Sammy could sense that. Alfie knew all the times of the services and always had his brother in position when pious ladies and gentlemen were coming out of church. Without Alfie, Sammy felt himself lost. He knew that it was morning, but he didn't know whether the church service had finished or whether the folk were still inside the building. There were no sounds of music or of praying voices either.

Sammy felt like being near to lots of people and staying there for as long as possible. The danger, thought Sammy, used to facing up to unpleasant facts, was to Alfie as well as to himself. If Mick handed him over to the man with the pistol, then neither his life nor Alfie's was going to be a very long one.

'Let's go over by the fountain,' he said to Mick. 'Should be nice and sunny there.'

'Lots of people around, too,' commented Mick in a carefree way – almost as though he had nothing on his mind but to get plenty of customers for Sammy. 'Let's go past the post office. They often put old squashed-up cardboard in that basket outside the door. I'll pick out two nice thick pieces for us to sit on. Bad for the bones,

Sammy my boy, sitting on cold, wet pavements! There's puddles everywhere after that flood last night.' He took a lot of care in steering Sammy through the crowd, stopping to fumble noisily in the post-office basket and triumphantly cracking the pieces of cardboard in Sammy's ear in order to show how dry they were. Perhaps his drunken mind had already forgotten the instructions from the mobster.

'You sit down in the sun and I'll stand,' said Sammy when he heard the splashing of the fountain close beside him. He would sing better standing up and he wasn't tired. There were plenty of people around – not in a hurry, either – just chattering about the raid on the post office.

The usual hymns would not do for this crowd, decided Sammy, and he began to sing the song about the highwayman Dick Turpin, his daring raids and his black mare.

'*My bonny, black Bess!*' As Sammy's voice rose up high and clear he could sense the crowd moving in his direction and soon coins were thudding into the cap between his feet on the ground. By the time he had sung the rollicking melody three times, his throat was dry. He bent down, fumbled in the cap, sorted through the pennies, thruppenny pieces, groats and sixpences and then handed Mick two of the large, round pennies.

'Get yourself a drink, Mick,' he said. 'I'll be all right here until you come back.'

Mick took a while to come back. Sammy leaned against the edge of the fountain, his cap firmly between his feet, and his fingers beating out the rhythm of flying horse hoofs on the marble surround of the fountain as he sang. The crowd was around him still and by now they were joining in the chorus.

When Mick arrived he joined in too. His voice had been made husky by alcohol, but he had the remnants of a singer about him and the crowd, now in a very good mood, applauded.

Perhaps Tom and Mutsy will come soon, thought Sammy. The sun had gone. He could feel the damp mist on his face and the raw, cold, sulphur-smelling stink of a London fog returning after a brief few hours of respite. Alfie never allowed him to do too much singing in the fog in case it spoilt his voice, but now his only safety lay in continuing to sing and continuing to attract people. Soon they would all be going away to get out of the fog and then the danger would come.

So Sammy sang every song that he could remember.

And the fog began to get worse.

'Here you are, old fellow, drink that beer. It's sour, and it's flat, but you won't mind that, will you?' The man handing Mick the beer sounded drunk himself. Probably just a passer-by who had had too much to drink, thought Sammy. The voice was not familiar and the accent was not that of a Londoner. Mick gabbled out his thanks and Sammy could hear him gulping down beer at breakneck speed as though he feared it would be snatched away from him. Sammy cheered inwardly. It sounded as if it was a good pint or even more. Mick would definitely be drunk after that – especially as he was drinking so quickly. He could hear the man's tongue searching around for the last drops and then the clatter of the pewter mug as it fell from his grasp.

Just let him lie down and go to sleep, prayed Sammy. He sensed that the last of the people listening to him had moved away. Now he was alone with Mick.

But the drink seemed to have given Mick courage instead of making him sleepy. His hand closed over Sammy's arm in a vice-like grip.

'Let's go,' he said and he began to drag the boy along the pavement.

'We're going in the wrong direction, Mick.' Sammy had a great sense of direction and knew that Mick was not taking him back towards St Martin's church and Bow Street, but to the opposite side of the square. He tried to keep his voice untroubled, but the grip on his arm was hurting him.

Mick didn't bother replying, just tugged harder. Sammy tried to resist. 'Don't, you're hurting me!' he shouted as loudly as he could. And then 'Help me, someone!' But even as the words were spoken he heard how muffled his voice sounded. The fog was getting thicker by the moment and there was no one left hanging around the fountains to hear him.

Mick, like Sammy's grandfather, had been brought up on a farm, and the muscles developed by digging and carrying heavy loads from an early age had stayed with him despite his age and the drink. He was far too strong for Sammy, who was dragged along unmercifully with his arm almost pulled out from its socket. Sammy shouted once more and then screamed, but his scream seemed to die away into the thickness of the mist.

And then he was released so suddenly that he fell to the ground.

There was a moment's silence. Then a great wail came from Mick.

'O merciful God in Heaven! My soul will go to hell. I've seen it. An apparition! It's in the Holy Book! The dead shall rise! Look! Look over there towards Whitehall! The dead are rising! Just under the devil's black horse! Old Jemmy is coming up from hell again. He's coming to get me! He's going to take me down there with him!'

CHAPTER 14

FLASH HARRY LOOKS FOR ALFIE

'Drunken fool,' muttered Alfie, pulling the lid of the manhole cover back down and then opening it again just a crack.

'C'mon, Jack,' he said after a moment, 'it's all right – it was just old Mick and he's scarpered. The fool will have forgotten all about us before he's gone fifty yards.' Cautiously, Alfie raised the iron cover a little higher and thrust his head out. There seemed to be no one else near. The fog was so thick that he could hardly see a hand in front of his nose. It was worth the risk. Rapidly he slid out and lay on the pavement. Jack followed and lay beside him for a moment. Both were out of breath.

'The statue of King Charles,' said Alfie after a moment. 'We're in Trafalgar Square!'

'No! Is it morning or night?' Jack sounded confused.

'Getting on towards evening.' Alfie didn't like to admit that he too was bewildered. It seemed like a lifetime since they had gone down into that sewer. He narrowed his eyes. The fog was coming down thickly now, soaking up all the wet from the streets into a choking cloud.

And then Sammy's clear voice said, 'Alfie, Jack.'

'Sammy?' Alfie was on his feet in a second, gaping in amazement and running headlong into the fog to find his brother pulling himself up from the ground, rubbing one arm. 'What are you doing here? What's happened to you? Where's Mutsy? And Tom?'

'That was just old Mick – had a bit too much beer,' Sammy informed them, ignoring his brother's questions. 'Thought he had seen Jemmy come up from hell.' He hesitated for a moment, but the bad news had to be told. 'There's one of Flash Harry's mob still after you, Alfie. He's got a gun. He wanted to keep hold of me until he could get his hands on you. Mick was taking me to him.'

'I'm a popular lad,' observed Alfie. 'Half of London seems to be looking for me. I know what they want . . .' He stopped and felt with his left hand inside his shirt front. It was no good, though; he knew that. His shirt and jacket had been torn when he'd pulled himself out of the manhole cover and now there was nothing there – not even a sodden piece of paper. 'Problem is, I've gone and lost it!' Oh, well, he thought. I remember what was on it, and perhaps it will make more sense to Inspector Denham than to me. The important thing now was to get Sammy home and out of danger.

'Let's get going, Sam,' he said. 'Take his other arm, Jack. Let's run. We need to get changed. All right by you, Sammy?'

With Alfie holding firmly to one arm and Jack to the other, running was one of the things that Sammy liked to do best. It was wonderful to go flying along without hesitating, without feeling his way tentatively, without worrying about bumping into anything. And the boys knew the way home so well that even the fog couldn't slow them down.

Jack and Alfie were both so wet that water was flying from them and, by the time they reached the top of Bow Street, Sammy was as wet as them. He didn't care, though. Two days ago Jack had collected plenty of coal from the riverbed. They would soon have a good fire going and Sammy had enough in his pocket to buy something for supper.

'Stop here,' said Alfie, suddenly coming to a halt. 'We should just check that none of my friends are waiting for me on Bow Street with a pistol in their pocket.'

'I'll go,' said Jack. 'They don't want me. They only want you.'

'Pity you can't let them know that you don't have the paper any longer,' said Sammy after Jack had gone. 'That's why they want you, isn't it? Perhaps you could ask the inspector to put a poster out describing it – that might work. Then Flash Harry and his mob will know you don't have it any more. It could say something like *Lost near Trafalgar Square* – what about that?'

'Why didn't I think of that? You're a lad with brains,' said Alfie, giving Sammy an admiring punch on the arm just as Jack came back to say that there wasn't a sign of any of Flash Harry's mob around, but there was one very cold policeman watching the cellar from across the road.

The policeman was the same man who had questioned them in Trafalgar Square, the night they found Jemmy's body. He looked very cold indeed, thought Alfie. A large drop of moisture hung from his prominent red nose.

'You going indoors?' he barked. 'Going to stay there, are you? No need for your personal guard any longer, what? I can tell Inspector Denham that you're all safely tucked up in bed, is that right?'

Without waiting for an answer, he strode off towards Bow Street police station, stamping his boots heavily on the pavement and swinging his arms, clapping himself loudly on the back in order to warm himself.

'Shame,' said Alfie with a grin as he took out the key to the cellar. 'It would have been good to have him standing outside our door all night.'

They had just finished changing their clothes and were piling more coal on the fire when the door to the cellar burst open and Mutsy raced in, licking Alfie, licking Jack, giving a quick wag of the tail and a touch of a wet nose in Sammy's hand and then going back to licking Alfie again. Tom and Sarah followed him.

'That dog's got a brain the size of a football,' said Alfie proudly. 'You don't need to tell him anything. He knows it all. He knows that I've been down the sewers. He don't need to learn to read, do you, Mutsy? His nose will tell him any story. And you needn't go sticking your nose in the air, Sarah. After all that floodwater, I don't stink of anything. I'm as clean as a baby after a bath. Wait till you hear all about it! How much did you get, Tom?'

'Four sixpences, two groats, one thruppenny piece and ten pennies,' said Tom proudly. 'Your board worked really well, Jack.'

'Three shillings and nine pence!' said Sammy wonderingly.

'Enough for the rent,' said Alfie. And then he took pity on Tom. 'And a slap-up supper!' he added.

'Is the board all right, Tom?' asked Jack anxiously.

'Cracked a bit,' said Tom. 'Big fat woman. Nothing would do her, but that Mutsy had to ride with her and rescue her if she fell in!'

'Thought she was crossing the River Thames, I suppose!' Although he was cold, tired, wet and bruised, Alfie could not help giggling at the thought of this fat woman crossing the puddles on Jack's board with Mutsy sitting demurely beside her like the guard on the stagecoaches.

'You'll have to rig up a sail next, Jack.' Tom was laughing so hard that tears were running down his face.

'Should have charged extra,' said Sammy. 'An extra groat for Mutsy to ride blunderbuss.'

'Let's have an early supper,' said Alfie after they had told about their adventures. 'That way, Sarah can have some before she has to go back to work. What do you think? Shall we have slices of salted beef? And a nice loaf of newly-baked white bread? What do you say, Tom?'

'I say yes,' said Tom. 'I'll go and get it. I earned it after all!' He grabbed the money from the table and went off.

Alfie rolled his eyes at Jack. 'Of course, *you* were the one who had the good idea and made the board, not him,' he said, but Jack just shrugged and Alfie said no more. He had too much else on his mind to be annoyed by Tom.

'We're thinking so much about Flash Harry and his mob of cracksmen that we've forgotten about the death of Jemmy,' said Jack after Sarah had told them how she visited Inspector Denham.

'Yes, Inspector Denham still says that's the root of the whole matter,' said Sarah.

'Well, I think that we need to make sure that Bert the Tosher had nothing to do with it first,' said Jack.

'And Opium Sal,' said Alfie. 'I'll question her tomorrow and you can talk to Bert, Jack.'

In his mind he felt that it wasn't too likely that Bert the Tosher had murdered Jemmy. After all, the whole affair of the gold cufflink was over and done with. What good would Bert do to himself by murdering Jemmy? He would just get himself hanged and leave his wife a widow and his children fatherless. In any case, thought Alfie, Inspector Denham was a smart man and if he felt that Jemmy's death was connected with the post office raid – well, the chances were that he was right.

And then he remembered Inspector Denham's advice to keep away from Flash Harry and his story about the man who ended up in the Thames with a lump of lead tied to his feet. Chances were that he was right about that, also!

CHAPTER 15

POLICE PROTECTION

As soon as Alfie had had some breakfast next morning, he went to see Inspector Denham. He had combed his rough curly hair carefully and put on the boots that Inspector Denham had given him money to buy. They were too big because he had got them so that they fitted Jack's feet as well, but they probably did make him look more respectable and might put the inspector in a good mood.

He needed the inspector if he was going to get through this affair without being knifed or shot.

'Next time I see a piece of paper flying through the air, I'll remember to let it fall into the gutter,' he said dramatically as soon as he was allowed into the inspector's room.

Inspector Denham looked up from the papers on his desk with a frown.

'What piece of paper?' he asked and then smiled at the sight of the large pair of boots.

'Well,' said Alfie, who loved to tell a good story. 'There I was standing over Jemmy's dead body, when Flash Harry himself came driving those post office horses across Trafalgar Square. He let this piece of paper drop, and I picked it up – and he saw me do it and ever since then he's been hunting me.'

'Where's the piece of paper?' asked the inspector eagerly, but Alfie shook his head.

'Probably down in the Thames with the flood water,' he said and then told the whole story of how he and Jack escaped by going down into the underground river under the cellar of the White Horse Inn and how the flood waters had swept them down until they managed to hold onto the wooden barrier gate.

'Well, you must be born to be hanged! You've had more lucky escapes in your short life than any man I know. Whatever was written on that piece of paper must be of vital importance to Flash Harry and his mobsters. You can read, can't you? You read it, I'm sure.'

Alfie nodded and then remembered Sammy's words. 'Would it be possible, sir, to put some sort of notice outside the police station to say that the piece of paper was lost – between Haymarket and Trafalgar Square? That's the truth, too. You see, sir, I can't put my mind to solving your murder while I'm being chased all over London by men with guns in their pockets.'

'I can see that.' The inspector nodded. He took a steel pen from a tray in front of him, dipped it in the ink bottle, rapidly wrote a few lines and then showed it to Alfie, ringing a small brass bell on his desk at the same time.

The red-nosed policeman came in immediately, scowling slightly at Alfie. 'Take this down to Monmouth Street, Constable,' said the inspector authoritatively, 'and get the printer to make half a dozen copies. Tell him that it's a rush job and that you'll wait until he has finished. Then put one outside this station, one in Trafalgar Square, one in Haymarket outside the White Horse Inn and the rest anywhere nearby. Be as quick as you can.'

The door had hardly closed behind the constable when Inspector Denham leaned across the desk and said, 'Tell me what was on the piece of paper.'

'Well, the paper itself was interesting,' said Alfie, who liked to tell a story in his own way. He eyed the man's impatient face and added sweetly, 'Very interesting.'

The frown was knitting the black bushy eyebrows again so Alfie continued quickly, 'You see, sir, it was toff's paper. Real thick stuff – very white – and that doesn't come cheap, does it? Very thick too, and with wavy bits around the edge, all done in gold.'

'Toff's paper,' murmured the inspector. 'Well, well, well, that's very interesting. Fits with what I was thinking. Tell me what was written on it.'

'Nothing,' said Alfie, but then, as he saw the disappointment in the man's eyes, he added slowly, 'but there was something drawn on it.'

'Drawn?' The inspector looked confused.

'Can't read, poor old Flash Harry, I bet. Not too bright.' Alfie pushed away the memory of how recently he had learnt to read himself. 'There was a picture of a moon and a clock beside it with the hands pointing to twelve – twelve at midnight, I suppose.'

'Hmm.' There was a disappointed note in the man's voice. 'Hardly seems worth all the fuss, does it?'

'There was a signature, too, though I couldn't read it – more a sort of scrawl at the bottom of the page. We thought that Flash Harry might use it for blackmail – getting money from the cove that wrote it.'

'Now that, I suppose, would make it worthwhile trying to recover it.'

There was a silence. The inspector shuffled papers on his desk and Alfie looked into the fire. It was a pity that he had taken the piece of paper from its hiding place and then lost it, but there was no use crying over spilt milk.

'I'll be going now, sir, unless you want me for something else.' Alfie rose to his feet. He knew what he was going to do with his day, but for the moment he didn't want to talk about it to the inspector. This was a job that he could manage better than any flat-footed policeman.

'I'll tell you something about that scrawl, sir,' he added. 'I'd say it were a toff that wrote it. Ordinary coves just print their name.' He noticed with satisfaction that the man looked more cheerful at that news.

'I still think it might have been someone from the post office that did it,' said the inspector as he slipped something from his pocket into Alfie's hand. 'The thing I can't make out, though, is why that old beggar man was murdered. That's the real mystery in this business. Solve that and we might solve everything else.'

Sarah was in the cellar when he got home. She smiled to herself as she heard Alfie coming down the steps, whistling. His interview with Inspector Denham must have gone well, or else given him ideas.

'Lumme, you've been tidying up here, haven't you,' said Alfie when he came in. Whenever Sarah felt nervous she always organised the boys into a clean-up.

'I can't think when there's a mess around me,' she said.

'Doesn't bother me,' said Sammy with a quiet smile.

'Not Mutsy, neither.' Alfie hugged the big dog exuberantly and placed the shilling that the inspector had given him into the rent box. Then he sat down beside the newly-cleaned window and told them about his talk with the inspector.

Sammy listened thoughtfully, then spoke. 'I was thinking that the link might be between Jemmy and the cove who drew the pictures. It might be nothing to do with Flash Harry.'

'Flash Harry wouldn't bother about someone like Jemmy,' Tom chipped in. 'Old Jemmy couldn't tell the police anything they didn't already know about Flash Harry and his mob.'

'I was thinking about that, too, Sammy,' said Alfie with a nod at Tom. 'But I don't suppose this toff who wrote the note, whoever he might be, was around that night, directing operations. There'd be no point in writing that note if he was going to be on the spot, unless he was just there secretly, of course.' A sudden idea occurred to him and he turned to Jack.

'Jack,' he said, 'could Jemmy read?'

'Yes, he could,' said Jack readily. 'I was telling him about going to the Ragged School and how I was getting on well with my reading and then he got a bit down and told me that he and his brother had both learnt to read and write before their mother died, and that the only good it did him these days was that he was able to write down Opium Sal's orders for drugs.'

'Opium Sal,' said Sammy thoughtfully.

Alfie punched his brother on the arm. 'That's what I'm thinking too. It's not just sailors, lascars and such like, who take opium. You get toffs there too. What do you say that a toff, perhaps someone working at the post office who was in league with the robbers, wrote the note down there in Opium Sal's place – safer than at the post office? Perhaps Jemmy saw him . . .'

'Saw the name of Flash Harry on the envelope.' Sarah was starting to look excited.

'And then when Mr Unknown Toff was walking through Trafalgar Square, just strolling around to see everything was going well, Jemmy saw him . . .'

'And put two and two together . . .' finished Jack. 'Jemmy was a clever fellow. I told you that, didn't I?'

'And the toff raises his stick and hits him on the head.' Sammy looked a bit doubtful. 'But that would be a great risk, wouldn't it? To do it right in the middle of all the crowds. Wouldn't it be more sensible to get Jemmy another time – perhaps at Opium Sal's place?'

'I think Sammy is right,' declared Sarah. 'I can't see a toff behaving like that. They've got too much to lose, these fellows with money and good positions. If anyone murdered Jemmy on the edge of Trafalgar Square like that – well, I'd say it would be Flash Harry or one of his mob. They don't care. They have so many hiding places that they can get out of the police's way in minutes and be running along a roof, or down a cellar. Once they get into St Giles or Devil's Acre they're safe. No one in those places would dare to squeal to the police.'

'I've thought of something else,' said Jack. 'I don't think that hole in Jemmy's forehead looked like it were done with a stick. More like something really heavy rammed into him. I remember seeing the bones pointing backwards.'

'Well,' said Alfie, 'we'd better get to work. The thought of that ten-pound reward makes me hungry. Even a quarter of it would make us rich. We need all the information that we can get about how Jemmy spent the day – who he talked to and all that sort of thing. Jack, you do the fish market, Sammy and I will have a chat with as many of the other beggars in Trafalgar Square as we can find. Tom, you try the street sweepers. They often know something.'

'What about the place that he dossed down in?' asked Tom.

'I haven't forgotten,' said Alfie. 'As soon as it's dark I'll go down to Opium Sal's place and have a few words with her. I have a feeling that the solution to the mystery is there.'

'Don't go down to that opium den on your own,' said Sarah with a shudder. 'You never know with people who take opium. They're fine when they have it and then after a few hours they need it again and they turn violent. They say Opium Sal would rob or murder to get the money for it. A girl I knew at the Coram Fields place – her mother took opium; she had to have it or she got the shakes, or else started screaming. Patsy told me that it costs more than a week's wages to buy a thimbleful – imagine that!'

Alfie could imagine. His father had owned a thimble to fit over his finger when he was stitching the heavy leather of shoes and the boys' grandfather used to tell Sammy stories about it being a cup for the fairies. It would only have held a half-teaspoon of the powder.

'Take Jack with you,' said Sarah. 'Opium Sal's place could be dangerous.'

CHAPTER 16

OPIUM SAL

When Alfie set off that evening, once the supper of steak and kidney pie had been eaten and reports had been made, it was Sammy, not Jack, that he took with him.

Alfie was fond of Jack, but Sammy was his brother and Alfie had a good opinion of Sammy's brains. And, of course, Sammy could hear things that were left unsaid, could reproduce any voice that he heard, remember the exact words said, and analyse things afterwards. So far they had made little progress in this puzzling matter. Alfie hoped that tonight would give them some new leads.

Alfie would have liked to have taken Mutsy, as well – he always felt safer when the big dog was with him – but that was impossible. Opium Sal would be terrified of him and some of her customers might be out of their minds and see the dog as a demon or some creature of their nightmares.

The church bells were ringing nine o'clock when the two of them set out, walking down St Martin's Lane, across Trafalgar Square, and then turning into Hungerford Lane.

Apart from the prosperous fish market opposite Trafalgar Square, Hungerford was a terrible place. There was a network of narrow, badly-lit lanes, and between them were dozens of small courts, each lined with tumbledown houses.

Alfie knew the place well and led Sammy without hesitation through the rabbit warren of lanes until they came to a narrow gateway leading to a courtyard that looked even worse than the surrounding ones.

'Terrible place,' he said to Sammy in a whisper. 'Worse than any of the others. Covered in filth and rusty old pots and pans. And Opium Sal's house is the worst of the lot. Don't know why old Jemmy dossed down here.'

'Never could keep a civil tongue in his head,' said Sammy. 'No one else would have him. I wonder why Opium Sal let him stay. Jack said he heard her cursing him one day as she passed and Jemmy cursed her back, even worse.'

'She was so out of her mind most of the time that probably she didn't know if he were cussing her or blessing her, or even the other way around,' agreed Alfie with a chuckle. 'But then you'd have to ask yourself why Sal wanted him in the first place. Jemmy wouldn't have been able to pay anything much in the way of rent – he didn't get much, just sitting there under that horse in Trafalgar Square from morning to night. Most of the time he didn't speak to the people passing, or even hold out his hand. That's not the way you get money from the pockets of the toffs. They like value for their pennies.'

'I'd say that Sal asked him to stay for protection,' said Sammy. 'He was a good fighter, was Jemmy. Some of Sal's customers could turn nasty when she was trying to get them out, when they had no more money to spend but they were still crying for the drug. Jemmy could come in handy in a case like that.'

'Perhaps we should have brought Mutsy after all,' said Alfie thoughtfully.

There was a Chinese man standing at the door of one of the houses in the court. Alfie knew him as Chinaman Jim – probably not his real name, but that's what he was called in the lanes of Hungerford. He was a rival to Sal and he watched them with narrowed eyes as they went towards Sal's door.

Alfie tried a knock, but there was no answer, so he pushed the door open and stepped inside. There was a tiny room to one side of the small hallway – more like a dog kennel than a room. That was where Jemmy had slept – Alfie had once walked back with him there. Its door was wide open and the few belongings Jemmy had were all pulled out of the chest and strewn around the floor.

'Seems like someone's been after something that Jemmy kept hid. Whoever came looking even took a knife to his mattress – there's bits of flock lying all over the place,' said Alfie in a whisper to Sammy.

'Police?' queried Sammy.

'Could be . . .' Alfie doubted it, though. The police would have been a bit tidier, he thought. 'More likely one of the opium smokers,' he added.

'Let's go upstairs,' said Sammy in a low voice.

Alfie kept a firm grip on his brother's arm as he led him up the worn stairs which tilted crazily to one side. All of these houses here at Hungerford seemed to be sliding into the oozy, black mud that lay alongside and beneath the River Thames.

'Might have to scarper quickly if things get a bit rough,' he said into his brother's ear.

The room they entered was long and low, with a few

rags of curtains dangling over the dirt-encrusted windows. It seemed a small room at first because it was crammed with beds, most of them broken and dipping to floor level at one corner or another. Beside each bed burned a small oil lamp and the room was full of heavily-perfumed brown smoke that rose to ceiling height.

Only three of the beds were occupied at the moment. One held a sailor, one Opium Sal herself and on the third was stretched a well-dressed gentleman with dark brown whiskers and thick, bristly eyebrows, his shining boots sticking out from the bottom of the filthy mattress. He held a long metal pipe in one hand and a stream of thick, brown smoke rose up from it. From time to time, he stretched out a gloved hand and rested the bowl of the pipe on the flame of the oil lamp and then brought the pipe back to his mouth, inhaling the smoke deeply into his chest. He looked vacantly at the two boys and began muttering to himself – just a stream of words which made no sense.

Opium Sal was wide awake, though. She put down her pipe and tried to get to her feet, but failed, pulling back her lips and displaying a few brown, rotting teeth in what seemed to be an attempt at a smile. Alfie reached out a hand and pulled her to her feet. Her skin was boiling hot and oozed moisture. As soon as she was upright, he took his hand away and rubbed it on the seat of his trousers.

'Come outside, Sal,' he said coaxingly. She was at the drowsy, contented stage, he saw, and that was good. Once she started to shake you couldn't do much with her.

She followed him quietly. The well-dressed gentleman began to mutter again. Alfie stopped for a second, but it was only a string of words about times and it made no sense, so he moved on, carefully shutting the door once all three of them were on the landing.

'Were you looking for me, Sal?' he asked. 'You were peeping in the window of our place on Bow Street.'

She looked puzzled for a moment, her eyes rolling vacantly, and Alfie hoped that she was not going to go into a fit. That happened to her sometimes. Once he'd pulled her from the middle of the road when she'd fallen down, foaming at the mouth and kicking her legs. She had been thankful to him for that and he wondered whether she still remembered.

'You knew Jemmy, didn't you?' she said suddenly. 'He was a friend to you boys, wasn't he?'

'That's right, Sal,' said Alfie soothingly. 'But tell us about that toff in there. He come here often?'

'Don't say that! Don't say that. No one must know. He don't like watchers. Don't watch him, that's a good boy. Don't tell the post office, whatever you do! Let me go now. I must have a pipe. I must have a pipe before my gentleman wakes up. Seven shillings he owes me. I must stay awake.'

By now she was shaking so badly that Alfie opened the door quickly and waited until she had reached her bed. He stood there for a minute looking at her as her trembling hands seized the metal pipe and shoved it over the flame of the oil lamp.

'Miracle she doesn't burn the place down,' whispered Alfie into Sammy's ear, but Sammy's attention was on the toff.

The man with the thick, dark eyebrows was muttering again. 'There's the bell. It's midnight. Must go.' And then, quite suddenly, he sat up, allowing the glowing pipe to fall to the ground. Sammy jumped as the man's shriek seemed enough to split the rotting ceiling overhead.

'No! I'll beat your head in, Jemmy, you villain, if you play tricks on me! Don't change the hands of the clock. I'll kill anyone who changes the time.'

CHAPTER 17

BY THE RIVER

Alfie was glad to get out of the opium den. The smell from the smoke was beginning to make him feel light-headed. He hurried Sammy along as fast as he could, pushing his way through the foggy lanes until they reached the broad, open space of Trafalgar Square. There were more gas lamps here and they seemed to thin the fog into a misty golden haze.

Alfie paused and drew in a deep breath. He was beginning to feel better. He stopped under one of the gas lamps and looked at Sammy. His brother seemed lost in thought so Alfie said nothing; just waited.

'That's three mad people raving about Jemmy,' said Sammy eventually.

'Three?' queried Alfie.

'Mick was raving about him rising up from hell and riding a black horse. Sal was raving about him being our friend. And then this other geezer, the toff with the bristly eyebrows and the pipe full of opium; he's going on about Jemmy being a villain and about clocks. We won't get any more sense out of him, especially if he stays there all night, and Sal hasn't any sanity left in her head, so that just leaves Mick. Might be worth talking to Mick when he's sober.'

'I don't care about Jemmy all that much,' protested Alfie. 'It's the post office robbery that I'm interested in. I'm only investigating Jemmy's death because Inspector Denham thinks that they are connected. Not sure that he's right, myself.'

'Interesting how that toff was going on about Jemmy altering the hands of the clock, wasn't it? And Sal talking about the joke played on Jemmy,' said Sammy, ignoring Alfie's protestations.

'What do you mean?' Alfie sounded reluctantly interested.

'Clocks would have been important in that robbery, wouldn't they?' pursued Sammy. 'From what you say, the whole thing went by split-second timing. Everything had to be in place to start when the fire was lit in Morley's Hotel.'

'Makes sense,' said Alfie. He thought about it for a moment. 'But I don't suppose that Jemmy actually changed the hands on a clock,' he said slowly. 'That opium muddles their brains. Maybe it wasn't a real clock the toff was thinking of – maybe it was him that drew the clock on the piece of paper I found. He might have been worried that Jemmy had seen him draw it . . .'

Sammy was nodding vigorously. 'So the toff had some inside knowledge about the jewels, and he was telling the robbers. Opium Sal mentioned the post office – could be he works there, knew about the jewels . . .'

At that moment a large hand was placed on Alfie's shoulder. He spun around, startled, then grinned and said, 'Bert! You gave me a fright, thought you was a copper!'

But there was no smile on Bert's face. 'Hear you get on well with coppers,' he said heavily. 'There's a little bird what told me you was seen coming up from the sewer at Whitehall. Don't you try to fasten Jemmy's death on me. You know what they say about the sewers, don't you? *Great place to get rid of man or beast.* So don't you go mentioning my name in Bow Street police station – not if you know what's good for you. Now get out of here, go on: scarper!'

Alfie did not argue. Bert the Tosher had the reputation of being a dangerous man and he wasn't going to tempt him into any violent action.

'I'd nearly decided to scrub him off my list,' he said in a low voice to Sammy, once they were a couple of streets away. 'Did you think he sounded guilty?'

'More scared-like,' said Sammy. 'Probably everyone is talking about Jemmy's murder and there would be quite a few people remembering the big fight that Bert had with him. Didn't sound that guilty to me.'

'Don't think we'll go home for a while, though. Bert mightn't know that we live in Bow Street and he might think we were popping in to the police station to see our policeman friend about him.' His brother might be right, but Alfie was cautious. In his experience, it wasn't always the most likely person who committed the crime. Briskly, Alfie towed Sammy in the opposite direction.

'You're not going back to Opium Sal's are you?' asked Sammy. His voice sounded more resigned than worried.

Alfie grinned. 'Blessed if you don't beat it all,' he said. 'How did you know that I was going towards Hungerford?'

'I can smell the river and the market,' Sammy replied. 'Anyway, why are you going?'

'Just thought of a question and of a man who could answer it,' returned Alfie. Sammy shrugged his shoulders and allowed himself to be led downhill towards the river.

When they reached the small court where Opium Sal

had her den, Chinaman Jim was still standing there outside his own door with his hands stuck into his sleeves and his eyes alert for any new customer. It was said that Jim employed an old sailor, addicted to opium, to attend to the customers and Jim himself never touched the drug, keeping out of the smoke-filled atmosphere.

'You have customer for me?' he asked Alfie, his eyes sharp and penetrating.

'No, but I can find you some,' said Alfie. 'How much you charge for a pipe?'

'Eight shillings a pipe, very clean room, very luxury,' said Chinaman Jim, eyeing Alfie keenly.

'All right if we go up – just for a minute? I'll need to tell the customers that I've seen the place.'

Alfie could feel himself being scrutinised intently for a moment and then the man nodded to him to follow and led them upstairs.

The stairs themselves were almost as bad as those at Opium Sal's, but the room was very much better, with even an attempt at comfort. Old, half-threadbare pieces of velvet were thrown over the bunks that lined the walls and the window was curtained in the same fabric. The bunks were hung with short velvet drapes and it was hard to see the customers. But plumes of brownish smoke floated around the ceiling and the room was filled with the same crazy mutterings.

Alfie did not linger. He gave a quick nod and headed downstairs again, hearing Jim's soft slippers pattering behind.

'Not a bad place,' he said briskly when he arrived back into the foggy atmosphere of the courtyard. 'Eight shillings is dear, though; Sal only charges seven, but I'll do my best for you.'

'That woman!' Chinaman Jim gave a scornful laugh.

'She gets plenty of customers, though,' said Alfie, seizing the opportunity. 'Toffs, too. Saw one in there to-night. You must see him go in and out – small fella with dark brown whiskers and thick eyebrows.'

'Him! Poor man! He is ashamed of himself. Hides his face with a newspaper when he comes.' Chinaman Jim had an odd, high-pitched laugh, but his eyes were sharp and clever.

Alfie hoped that he had sounded sufficiently casual and had not aroused any suspicions. 'I reckon he's a great customer for Sal,' he remarked carelessly. 'Stays there all night, I suppose.'

'Never stays long,' hissed Chinaman Jim. 'You watch. He'll come out any minute now. One pipe only. You see.'

Alfie nodded. That fitted with what he was thinking: that Bristly Eyebrows probably didn't take too much opium, if he managed to hold down a job at the post office. It would be interesting to follow him and find out where he went when he left Opium Sal's place.

'Not much of a customer, then. Now what's my share in all this? If I bring a customer, it won't be just to put a smile on your face, old fellow. What's in it for me?'

Sammy bit back a chuckle. Old Alfie was a great actor, he thought. Anyone would swear he had lost interest in the toff with the bristly eyebrows by the way he immediately began to bargain for a fee of thruppence for every customer he brought. He could just imagine the look of disgust on Alfie's face as he contemptuously turned away at the offer of a penny.

'You bring, I see,' shouted Chinaman Jim as Alfie took his brother by the arm and walked away. Alfie did not reply and Sammy knew that not only had his brother no intention of supplying customers for opium dens, but now that he had got the information that he was looking for, the man was of no further interest to him.

'We'll wait on the far side of the gate of the court,' said Alfie in his ear. 'Don't suppose Bristly Eyebrows even noticed us when we were in Opium Sal's place, but there's no sense in running risks.'

Sammy was just beginning to feel chilled in the damp, foggy air when Alfie breathed in his ear. 'Here he comes.'

The man turned up towards the Strand and stood for a moment under the light of the gas lamp with the air of someone who was not sure which way to go. He was a small, thin man of about fifty, very well dressed in a black tail coat and a shirt with a stiff white collar.

Alfie inspected him carefully. Something glinted from the man's collar. Alfie dropped Sammy's arm and cautiously moved nearer, being sure to keep within the shadow of the gate. Yes, he was right – there was something there!

There on the man's collar was a small badge made from three entwined gold letters. After a minute of staring, Alfie made them out. GPO was what they were: General Post Office! So Sammy had been right!

All of the post office workers wore badges, but the ordinary workers' badges were made from cheap tin and painted red. This fellow must be something high up, probably an inspector or something. But that was not all. Alfie remembered the note that he had picked up in Trafalgar Square – it had those same tangled-up letters woven into the expensive paper in gold. With a satisfied nod, Alfie moved back to Sammy and took his arm again.

'Hang on a minute,' he whispered to Sammy. 'I'll just let him get ahead and then we'll follow.'

But the man did not go down the Strand as Alfie had

expected. After a minute he turned and began to go in the opposite direction, downhill, followed at a distance by the boys. He was staggering now and his pace was dead slow.

'Going towards the river,' whispered Alfie in Sammy's ear. 'He's reeling and lurching just like he's drunk.'

Sammy listened to the uneven footsteps, but he could hear something else as well. The man was breathing as though he had been climbing a steep hill, sucking in great mouthfuls of air.

'Coming out by the river, now,' whispered Alfie.

He sounded nervous, thought Sammy. Normally Alfie would not have bothered saying that. He would have known that Sammy would feel the damp air of the river on his face after emerging from that narrow lane enclosed by tall houses.

'What's he doing?' Sammy whispered back.

'He's not going on the bridge; he's just standing by the river and gulping. Hope he's not going to throw himself in.' Alfie sounded annoyed and added in a low whisper: 'I suppose I'd have to go in after him if he did or I'd never know if he had anything to do with Jemmy's death and that robbery. Come on. He's half out of his mind. I'll talk to him.'

Quickly he towed Sammy over towards the man. 'Penny for a blind boy, mister?' he said briskly in a loud voice.

'Wa . . . wa . . . a . . . min . . . must get air.' The man noisily gulped in mouthfuls of fog.

'You're not well,' asserted Alfie. 'Walk you back, sir. Where are you going?'

'The p . . . ose . . . toffice . . .' slurred the man.

Post office! Alfie translated the broken syllables in his mind and felt a tremor of excitement rush through him. This confirmed his suspicions. He had known of many people addicted to opium and, rich or poor, they had one thing in common. They would lie, steal or even kill to get money for their drug. It looked as though this man with his fancy post office badge did have something to do with the raid on the post office. Perhaps Alfie would be able to get out of him where the jewels were hidden and Alfie's gang would be able to claim the ten-pound reward after all.

The man produced a snowy white handkerchief from his pocket and began to mop his face. The river air seemed to be doing him good. His breathing had slowed down and the incoherent muttering had stopped.

'Little blind boy,' he said and his voice was almost normal. 'You've got hair like a little angel in heaven.'

'Thank you, sir,' said Sammy calmly. He was used to that sort of thing, but usually from pious old ladies outside churches.

Bristly Eyebrows swung suddenly around to Alfie.

'Take him away,' he hissed. 'There's evil in the air here. Don't you smell it? Take him away immediately. Here,' he fumbled in his pocket and produced a coin. Alfie caught a glimpse of silver as the coin glimmered in the light from a nearby gas lamp.

'Just going, sir,' he said reassuringly. He knew what these opium smokers were like – took little or nothing for them to throw a fit of hysterics.

'We'll wait here for a while and then when he's forgotten all about you I'll go back down and see if I can get some sense out of him,' he whispered to Sammy once they had withdrawn into the dim opening of Hungerford Lane.

'Wonder why he chose to come down to the river?' whispered back Sammy. 'If he always just takes one pipe, you'd think he would go home afterwards.'

'Perhaps he comes down for the air. It seems to be doing him good. He's walking up and down, now. Hang on a minute and I'll have a chat with him before his senses come back completely.'

Alfie strolled back towards Bristly Eyebrows. 'So you work at the post office in Trafalgar Square, do you?' he asked briskly and held his breath while the man turned his head towards him.

'That's right.'

Alfie relaxed as soon as he heard the tone of the man's

voice. It was mellow, a bit fogged up – just right for getting information out of him. 'That was a good trick that you pulled off, getting them jewels as well.' He gulped nervously. Was he laying himself open to being killed? Still, he told himself, opium smokers were famous for not remembering anything that was said while they were still dopey with the drug. At least the man showed no interest in his words, just continued to gaze up the river. Alfie went on rapidly, 'Shame about old Jemmy getting that bash on the head – killed him, you know. Still, I suppose he was asking for it, wasn't he? Spying on you all? Asking for money? Or was it the post office raiders killed him? Maybe he got in their way?'

'No!' The man suddenly sounded more normal, just as if he were startled out of his opium dreams. 'No, nobody touched Jemmy. I saw him myself, after the raid, when I was going home. He was talking to one of the engineers from Birmingham, the fellows that were examining the pump for the fountains.'

'But . . .' began Alfie and then stopped. There was a low whistle from Sammy and then his voice.

'Boat coming,' he whispered.

CHAPTER 18

WHERE ARE THEY?

The White Horse Inn had a reputation for good food and Sarah was busy serving breakfast to half a dozen tables when a voice said quietly in her ear:

'Any sign of those two scoundrels?'

'I'm not sure what you mean, sir,' said Sarah, neatly depositing the plate of sausages and eggs onto the small table in front of one of the Birmingham engineers while balancing the tray with his beer in her other hand.

Her heart thumped as she turned to see that it was the man with the red scarf. He still wore the scarf – it must be his trademark. Most of these flash thieves had something which made them stand out from the others.

'A sharp girl like you; I'm sure you must remember me.' The man's eyes were fixed intently on her. 'Came here the other night looking for a pair of young pickpockets,' he continued. 'You remember me now, don't you? Stole my watch, they did, the two of them. Worth a pound it was; that's a jailing matter. No wonder they're keeping away from me. But a smart girl like you might hear something. You could tell me where to find them. There's a shilling for you if you can tip me the wink. I'll be in here again tonight and I'll have that shilling in my pocket.'

'A shilling!' Sarah did not have to pretend to be surprised. A shilling was a lot of money for a little piece of information about two boys. She decided to probe a little more.

'Oh, yes, I remember you now. You went down to the kitchen to look for them, didn't you?' Sarah cleared some emptied tankards onto her tray. 'I'll have a word with the scullery maid and see if she knows anything.' She smiled at Red Scarf, trying to conceal her nervousness.

'And you're sure that you don't know them?' He was eyeing her narrowly with a shade of suspicion in his eyes.

'Well,' she said slowly. An idea had come to her. 'I can't talk here,' she whispered with a quick look over at the landlord who, luckily, was staring in her direction.

'I'll meet you at two o'clock in Trafalgar Square.'

'Too public,' whispered the man. 'Make it Monmouth Street, near to Seven Dials. You'll be able to bring the young fellows with you, won't you?'

Sarah nodded, gulping nervously. Seven Dials was a terrible place, full of criminals, murderers and cracksmen. She edged away from him.

'Sarah, take a tray up to number fifteen,' shouted the innkeeper, to her relief.

'Is he still sick, then?' she said, glad to find an opportunity to get away from the man with the red silk scarf and the penetrating eyes. 'He's very keen on his meals, for a sick man.'

'Who cares how much he eats? Go on, girl, none of your business,' said the innkeeper gruffly. 'He'll pay his bill on Saturday with the rest of them engineers before they go back to Birmingham. Nothing to us, if he eats his meals in the bar, or eats them in his bedroom.'

Nothing to *you*, thought Sarah. You're not the one that has to climb up and down three flights of stairs carrying heavy trays laden with food. Not to mention buckets of hot water in the morning so that the man could wash and shave. Still, at least the man in bed didn't drink like the rest of the engineers!

He doesn't *look* sick, she thought, although the words

'come in' in answer to her knock were just a croak. He never said much, never even thanked her, just lay on the bed with his face turned to the window.

'Here's your breakfast, Mr Batson.' Sarah did not expect a reply and she got none, though apparently Mr Batson did talk to the boot boy in a hoarse whisper and sent down orders and requests by him. She attended to the fire – it wasn't really her job, but the unfortunate scullery maid was very overworked and Sarah remembered what a dreadful task it was.

She would never want to be a scullery maid again, and she had resolved to do her work at the inn especially well. At first she had planned to stay only a few months and then to move on to a job in a private house, but now she found herself changing her mind. Private houses had bullying housekeepers and snobbish butlers and the owners of the houses despised their servants and treated them like slaves, expecting them to be at their beck and call for sixteen hours a day. Mr Pennyfeather, the landlord at the White Horse, was a bit grumpy sometimes, but she had a decent, well-furnished bedroom and was treated fairly.

And I do enjoy having time off every day, thought Sarah as she went down the stairs with the empty coal scuttle in one hand and the water pail in the other. The cook and the other servants were friendly, also.

'You doing anything special this afternoon?' asked Dora, the other parlour maid, when Sarah reappeared in the bar.

'I have to go and see a friend,' said Sarah promptly. She and Dora shared a bedroom and as they were the only parlour maids they had become friends. Sarah knew that Dora was going to suggest window-shopping in Oxford Street as usual, where they wandered from shop to shop planning the outfits that they would buy if they had the money. Sarah had enjoyed this for a while, but now she was getting tired of pretend shopping. Also, she had something else on her mind – the frightening man in the red scarf. She had decided to go and see Inspector Denham again.

Almost as though he had read her thoughts, the man turned around, gave her a wink and raised his glass to her. Sarah forced her lips to a polite smile, slipped rapidly behind the bar and began vigorously polishing the beer taps and wiping the counters clean of all the circles from the mugs and tankards.

As soon as Sarah had finished clearing the plates from the parlour, she set off for Bow Street police station.

As she had hoped, Inspector Denham was in his office when she arrived. He was very nice, thought Sarah, as she sat in the chair that he pulled out for her. He spent a few minutes asking about her new job and whether she was happy in it, and then she told him about the man with the red silk scarf.

'He's after Alfie and Jack,' she said. 'He tried to catch them two nights ago, just before the storm broke. He chased after them to the White Horse Inn, but they managed to get away.' Sarah decided not to tell the inspector about the boys going down the sewers. That might be against the law. 'And then he turned up today at the White Horse again, trying to get out of me whether I knew them. I told him that I would bring Alfie and Jack to Seven Dials at two o'clock,' she finished. 'You might be able to capture him then.'

'Unlikely,' said the inspector wearily. 'That place is full of criminals. I'd need twenty men to go in there and the chances are that by the end of it all, I'd have a man shot or badly injured and no one would be captured.' He saw her disappointment and added kindly, 'But you would be of great use to us. We're beginning to suspect that there might be two gangs involved. We know that Flash Harry's gang is one of them, but this affair seems a bit clever for them.' He stopped for a minute, thinking hard. 'Would you be able to describe this man for someone I know?' he asked. 'This chap is very clever with his pencil and he might be able to make a drawing of him.'

Sarah nodded.

Inspector Denham left the office briefly and, five minutes later, a constable appeared with a man in a floppy hat with a satchel tucked under his arm.

Inspector Denham ushered the artist into his office and firmly shut the door on the policeman, but when the picture was finished and the artist had been paid and thanked, he invited the constable and another policeman in. Sarah watched their faces light up with excitement.

'Sid the Swell!' exclaimed PC27. 'He's got him dead to rights – good as if he sat for his portrait!'

'That's him, all right,' commented PC32. 'Do you see the way his nose turns to one side? He got that broken nose from the night watchman at the jewellery place in Burlington Arcade.'

'Deals in jewels, does he?' mused the inspector. 'Well, well, well, now that's interesting.' He saw Sarah looking at him inquisitively and gave a nod.

'There was a registered package of diamonds among the mail that was stolen from the Trafalgar Square post office,' he said to her. Sarah nodded. She knew this already. 'The jewels were being sent from a diamond merchant in Hatton Garden to an address in Holland. It seems likely that the raid was planned specially for that night because the thieves knew about the diamonds – I suspect someone from the post office itself gave them the information. It was a hugely valuable parcel – we are trying to get hold of it before it's shipped abroad for the best price that can be got for it.'

'And nothing has been found yet, has it?' asked Sarah, thinking of the ten-pound reward that was still on the board outside the police station. She would use her share of the reward to go back to school, she thought. She would like to be more educated. The Ragged School, which was free, had been burned down, but there were other schools if you had the money to pay for them.

'Shall we put the picture outside the door with a "Wanted" sign on it, Inspector?' asked one of the constables.

'I don't think so,' said Inspector Denham after a pause. 'Sid the Swell on his own is not much good for us. We want to recover the diamonds, but above all I want to lay my hands on the traitor who tipped the gang off about what was in the Trafalgar Square mailbags that night. Thank you, Sarah; you've been very helpful, but I must ask that you leave this case to us now. And don't, whatever you do, meet with Sid the Swell this afternoon. Go back to the inn and stay safe. Constable, see Sarah out.'

'Leave it to us, now, Sarah,' said the constable in a

friendly voice as they stood together at the door of Bow Street police station. 'Don't start doing any investigations, not you nor any of the other kids. That Sid the Swell is a nasty piece of work. Best not to meddle with him.'

CHAPTER 19

BRISTLY EYEBROWS

Alfie and Sammy had retreated to the shadows at the top of Hungerford Bridge.

The river was very still, very silent, the weight of the heavy fog smothering all sounds. Alfie listened. For a moment he heard nothing but then a sound came, from under the bridge. It was unmistakably the clank of a chain being stealthily drawn through the water. And it was not the only sound.

Sammy was right. There was a boat there, also. Alfie could hear it drift in the water, occasionally bumping softly against the iron support of the bridge. It must have just glided up the river on the ebbing tide. The faint murmur of whispering voices came to him and then a short, hissed '*Sh-sh-sh*' from one of them.

The chains clonked again, then came the sound of something large being hauled over the side of the boat. One man groaned softly with the effort of pulling it in. A second, unwieldly bulk was loaded into the boat in the same way. Then the sound of the chain being dragged in.

Suddenly the truth flashed on Alfie. On the night of the robbery, the post office raiders had driven off at high speed down Hungerford Lane. A couple of the gang must have jumped from the wagon with the mailbags and hidden them under the bridge, while the others led the police on a wild goose chase across the river. That was it, he thought. Tonight they were pulling the mailbags up and taking them away.

Where would they go? Would it be possible to follow them? The river bank was very dark and the fog was coming down thickly. Even without Sammy, it would be impossible for Alfie, running on the dark shoreline, to keep up with a boat rowing downstream on an ebbing tide. Alfie froze in an agony of indecision. The thought of losing that ten-pound reward made him want to scream with frustration.

The boat slid out from under the bridge. Just one man

was sculling, moving the oar as silently as possible, towards the Hungerford Stairs where the Bristly Eyebrows stood, still muttering to himself. A second man reached out a hand and held him firmly while he stepped into the boat. No one spoke. It seemed this was not the first time they had seen him in this state. The boat moved back into the shadow of the bridge and Alfie could see nothing more. Then, quite suddenly, the toff began to sing in a strange, high-pitched voice.

'Hickory Dickory Dock,
The mouse ran up the clock,
The clock struck . . .'

Then there was a sort of groan.

And then silence.

The boat moved away; the men rowing strongly and smoothly down the Thames. Alfie let go of Sammy's arm and went cautiously down towards the river's edge, being careful to keep in the black shadow of the nearby boathouse. By now, the boat was well out into the middle of the river, going downstream towards the sea. And there was no sign onboard of Bristly Eyebrows.

He must be with them, thought Alfie, though when he looked out towards the moonlit boat he could still only see two heads.

Then both heads looked all around, as if they were

making sure that no one else was near. And a minute later, Alfie knew why.

A large, heavy object was heaved over into the water, making a surprisingly small splash. 'My God,' thought Alfie, 'they must have strangled Bristly Eyebrows!'

Alfie held his breath, praying that they could not see him. He did not dare to move until the boat was far downstream, the men rowing quickly as if to get away as fast as possible from the object that they had thrown into the Thames.

Alfie felt himself filled with anger as he went back and whispered to Sammy what had happened. For the first time, the ten-pound reward faded from his mind. That poor old fellow, he thought. Wouldn't have done it if he hadn't needed the money for his opium drug. He seemed a harmless old cove. He certainly had not been the one to kill old Jemmy. He wasn't big enough, or strong enough. Probably always had the shakes!

But Flash Harry and his gang – they were a different matter. The sooner Inspector Denham caught them, the better.

And then came a voice. Someone was coming down Hungerford Lane – two people, one talking to the other.

'Ever eaten smoked eel, Jack?' said the voice. 'Real

delicacy, that. Stick it up the chimney and leave it there for a few months. Tastes great!'

It was Charlie Higgins, the fisherman, and he had Jack with him. Now Alfie could make out their figures, each carrying a pair of oars. If Charlie was willing to help, then they could follow the boat and see where the raiders went.

Alfie had a short struggle with himself. If they used Charlie's boat, and Charlie's rowing power, they would have to share the reward with him – at least. He might even claim three-quarters of it!

However, without a boat, the men would not be traceable. Alfie made up his mind. The important thing now was to catch this gang before they did any more harm.

'Stay there,' he whispered to Sammy and slipped quietly back up towards the two figures coming down Hungerford Lane.

Jack always said that Charlie Higgins was a clever fellow and it turned out to be true. After a few words from Alfie he understood the situation completely and continued to discuss the smoking of eels in loud, carrying tones, as he and Jack came out from the darkness and stopped beneath the one solitary gas lamp at the top of the Hungerford Stairs. They dragged the heavy wooden boat down the bank and launched it into the river. Jack held the boat as steady as he could by gripping the iron bar of the Hungerford Stairs while Alfie helped his brother into the boat.

'Sort out the fishing lines, Jack. Blessed if they aren't all in a tangle.' Charlie's voice boomed over the silent water. By now Charlie and the three boys were well out into the centre of the river, quite a distance from the Hungerford shore.

Alfie lay flat down on the floor of the boat and allowed no more than his forehead and eyes to appear over the side. Sammy sat peacefully in the centre of the craft and in the prow Charlie, with a voice like a foghorn, cursed Jack for being so slow with untangling the lines and declared his intention of moving off before the tide turned.

'That's the time to catch eels, sonny boy,' he roared. 'If I have to hang around here any longer there won't be a single one of them critters left to catch. They don't sit on their backsides and hold up little placards saying *Please catch me!* you know.'

'Yes, Mr Higgins,' said Jack respectfully. He seized a pair of oars and with a strong, steady stroke kept time with Charlie.

Charlie was still bellowing, but even without that,

they would probably not have heard a sound from the galley boat just ahead of them.

It was lucky that Charlie Higgins liked the sound of his own voice. Between the bridges of Hungerford and Waterloo he never stopped giving his opinions on fishing and fish markets, and telling stories about fish sellers he had known during half a century on the river. He kept well to the south side of the galley boat that they were following and only a few feet behind it. It would be impossible for the men to land the boat without being spotted. And as they'd just killed a man, it was unlikely that they wanted to draw attention to themselves.

'Drop back a little and we can watch to see where they go,' whispered Alfie into Charlie's ear when they reached Southwark Bridge, and the man nodded.

'Let's cast a line here, lad, and see if the eels are rising tonight,' he said in tones loud enough to be heard by the men in the boat. 'Come on boy, ship your oars,' he added to make it clear to anyone that might be listening that the fishing boat was going to stop.

The galley, however, did not stop. Nor did it go towards the shore. It continued on its journey, nearer to the south bank of the river than the north, but not so near that it looked as though it were going to land. After a couple of minutes, Alfie touched Charlie on the arm and murmured, 'We'd better follow them.'

'Gently with the oars, lad,' said Charlie in a hoarse whisper to Jack. 'Feather them lightly. There's no sense in calling attention to ourselves, now. Let them think that they've left us behind.'

The galley was going faster now, so fast that Charlie and Jack had to put all their strength into the sweep of their oars. The moon was completely shrouded in mist now, but Alfie just managed to keep the raiders' boat in his sights through the darkness. Were they going to lose the prize, after all?

They were heading towards London Bridge. The tide was ebbing fast and soon the large menacing bulk of the Tower itself loomed above them. Where was the galley going?

'Past London Bridge now,' he whispered in Sammy's ear.

'Bet you any money that they've got a hiding place down the East End,' whispered back Sammy.

Alfie relaxed. That made sense. The East End of London was a lawless place, a place where thieves had hideouts and where the proceeds of crimes were hidden. Sammy was probably right. The post office raiders must have their lair here. For a few minutes Alfie had been worrying that the galley was making for the open sea, perhaps to meet a steamer going to some foreign place – maybe India, he thought, remembering Mallesh, the young Indian boy who the gang had met and befriended not long ago.

'We'll just see where they go to and then go back and tell the police,' he whispered to Charlie and the man nodded. He must have been getting worried about losing his small fishing boat if they went among the large ships.

Around a bend in the river, on the south bank, there was a small inlet – a place where, when the river flowed more freely, ships could moor. Now it was a shallow, scummy, stagnant piece of water. There were corpses of rotting fish floating on its surface and the place smelt like a graveyard.

In the middle of the water was a small island. Alfie had seen terrible sights in London – St Giles was a dreadful slum and most of Hungerford was a nightmare of tiny, stinking lanes – but he had never seen or smelt anything as bad as these houses on Jacob's Island. They were built of wood and were all slipping into the water, with broken walls and roofs making most of them uninhabitable, even by the very poor. Privies, with broken doors or no doors at all, poured their filth down into the stinking water and lamplight from a gutted window illuminated a strange red fluid gushing out from one of the houses. Here and there, dead animals lay around, putrid and swollen.

The men in the galley boat did not hesitate, however. They crossed the festering water towards one of the houses. Someone had been waiting and watching for them. A rope was thrown out of a first-floor window with broken, rotting shutters. One of the men in the galley caught hold of it and then, to Alfie's enormous satisfaction, a sack was tied to the end of the rope and then hoisted slowly up.

'We've seen enough,' he said in a low voice. 'Let's get back before they feed us to the fishes.'

CHAPTER 20

A
MIDNIGHT SEARCH

Sarah was exhausted by the time midnight sounded from the nearby church bells. This was always the worst time of the day ever since the engineers from Birmingham had arrived. They had come to stay a week in London in order to look at the fountains in Trafalgar Square, so they could build as good a pump house back in their home city. They liked to walk around London in the evening, or else to go and see a play, and then they arrived back at the White Horse Inn in Haymarket – not tired, but hungry and above all thirsty.

The two parlour maids had been to and from the scullery to the bar forty times in each hour, fetching tasty things to eat; they had been pouring beer, bringing glasses, mugs and tankards back to the kitchen and fetching clean supplies. Sarah's legs ached, her ankles ached, her arms ached from carrying heavy trays but above all her head ached. And that was worst of all.

'Could you look after things here on your own for a few minutes?' she whispered in Dora's ear. 'If I don't get a breath of fresh air away from all this cigar smoke I think my head will split.'

'You go on, take ten minutes. The landlord has gone up to see that fellow Ned, that engineer that's sick in number fifteen. I think that he wants to make sure he will be out of here on Saturday morning with the rest of that crowd. He was talking about getting a doctor to see him.'

Sarah smiled her thanks and slipped out of the room. The man with the red silk scarf had not shown himself at the White Horse Inn again, but she continually looked out for him – afraid he would come for revenge after she had not turned up at the Seven Dials, afraid that he might have seen her go into the police station – and she thought that had probably helped cause her headache.

Quickly, she pulled on her black cloak. It was new – she had been saving for weeks to buy it – and it was thick and warm in the freezing fog of midnight. She went through the porch and stood outside the window of the bar for a few minutes.

There were sounds of merriment from inside the room. Someone was singing a comic song. And when that came to an end there were calls for another one.

'Ned!' Suddenly they were all shouting the name. 'Ned's the one that can sing! Get him out of bed! We want Ned!'

'He'd be no good to you. The man's still got such a sore throat that he can only whisper.' That was the landlord's voice.

So the landlord was back downstairs. I'd better go in, thought Sarah, sighing. She had been hoping to have a walk. Her headache was still bad but she wasn't being paid to take a breather outside. It was time for her to go back to work.

She had just turned to go through the door when a voice from out of the fog whispered, 'Sarah.'

Sarah stopped and peered through the mist. 'Is that you, Tom?'

'Yes, it's me. And Mutsy.'

'What's the matter?' asked Sarah.

'It's Alfie and Sammy. They haven't come home yet.'

'Where's Jack?' asked Sarah.

'He's gone out with Charlie Higgins – gone eel-fishing. I'm on my own.'

'What time did Alfie and Sammy go out?'

'About nine. They've been gone for three hours. They were going down to Opium Sal's. Alfie said that they'd be back in half an hour or so. I'm worried that something has happened.'

Sarah thought quickly. From within the White Horse Inn she could hear the landlord's voice.

'Drink up, gents,' he was shouting. 'Last orders now!' He, like his staff, was getting tired of the long hours that these engineers kept.

'I'll be out as soon as I can,' she whispered to Tom. 'Be back here in about ten minutes.' With a quick pat on Mutsy's head, she slipped back inside.

The landlord had gone into the bar when Sarah came upstairs ten minutes later, after delivering the last load of glasses, mugs and tankards to the scullery maid. Most of the late-night crowd were on their way to bed at last.

'Cover up for me,' she whispered to Dora who was just coming down. 'A cousin of mine is in a fix. I have to go and see about something.'

She crept downstairs again, taking her cloak from a nail in the scullery door. The bunches of keys for the inn hung there and Sarah carefully eased off one of them and put it into her pocket. The landlord was chatting to the barman and she slipped along the passageway, opening the heavy door just a crack and then closing it gently behind her.

Tom was in the very same place – Sarah had the impression that he had not stirred since she had seen him last. He was shivering and she began to walk fast in the direction of the river to try to warm him up. When his teeth continued to rattle, she put her cloak over his shoulders.

'Only for a few minutes until you warm up, so don't you start getting too attached to it,' she warned and was glad to see that he smiled slightly at that. As the youngest member of the gang he was not used to being left in charge.

'So he just took Sammy when he went to Opium Sal's place, is that right?' Sarah, also, was feeling a little worried. Why would Alfie be missing for three hours? He said that he just wanted to find out one or two things. Did this mean that the two boys were in bad trouble?

'Let's walk down there now,' she decided and as soon as they had crossed Trafalgar Square and entered Hungerford Lane, she gave the command, 'Find Sammy!' to Mutsy. Alfie had taught him this and the big dog had once saved Sammy's life by leading Alfie to where his brother lay.

Immediately, Mutsy put his nose to the pavement.

Down Hungerford Lane he trotted, picking out the scent of Sammy's feet unerringly from the stinks of rotting food and filth that lay around. At the gate to a small, grimy court of houses, the dog paused, lifting his nose high into the air and sniffing vigorously. It seemed impossible that he could smell Sammy here amongst the strong, pungent waft of opium smoke, but somehow he seemed to be able to tell that the blind boy was no longer there. Without hesitation, he turned away from the gate and began to track down towards the river. Sarah and Tom followed behind.

Why had Alfie gone down towards the river, wondered Sarah? Had he found out something from Opium Sal? Something about Jemmy, Sal's lodger? Or something about the post office raid? Were the two connected, as Inspector Denham thought? She accepted her cloak back from Tom, felt his hand to make sure that he was warm, and then went on thinking.

When they reached the river bank, Mutsy came to a full stop. He looked at Tom and then at Sarah. Sarah watched him anxiously. The big dog was looking downstream, down towards the distant lights of the Tower of London. Every fibre of his body seemed stiff and intent. He whimpered softly, gazing intently down the river.

And then, quite suddenly, he sat back on his haunches,

pointed his nose at the sky and howled, a terrible wail of loss and sorrow pouring out of his jaws.

Sarah stared at him. The hairs at the back of her neck prickled and despite her warm cloak, she shivered. Beside her she heard Tom gulp noisily.

Mutsy sounded like a dog who was mourning the death of his masters.

CHAPTER 21

UNDERGROUND

'Let's get out of here,' repeated Alfie uneasily. He kept his voice very low, although they were quite a distance from the house where Flash Harry and his men had moored their galley boat.

'No,' whispered Charlie Higgins obstinately. 'We'd look proper mugs if we got the police and they found that the birds had flown. Let's just get a bit nearer and make sure that they're bedded down for the night before we go for the police.'

Without waiting for an answer he picked up the oars and began to row towards Jacob's Island.

The house was very still – broken panes of glass

glinted in the pale rays of the moonlight. Charlie rowed a little nearer and then stopped, one large hand held to one ear. The three boys listened intently also. Alfie looked at Sammy, but Sammy said nothing. Charlie gave an exasperated click of his tongue.

'They're gone! The rats have scarpered! They must have dropped the loot then rowed off again!' His voice was a murmur compared to its usual volume, but Alfie gave an anxious glance at the house. Charlie was getting excited by the pursuit of the post office gang, and by the thought of sharing that ten-pound reward. He stared intently up at the broken shutters of the house then, without warning, he began to row vigorously towards the north side of the river.

'Should we follow them down river, or go to the police station near the Tower of London? That would be nearer than the one at Bow Street. What do you say, lads?' Charlie's voice was tense with excitement.

A second later, a shot rang out. It hit Charlie right in the centre of his head. He slumped to one side. Instinctively Alfie grabbed Sammy's arm and Jack grabbed the other. The boat rocked violently then tilted to one side. The body of the heavy fisherman slid over the side and hit the water with a great crash. The boat reared up and then toppled over.

For a moment Alfie did not know what had happened. A heavy weight struck him on the head; he was suffocating, drowning.

Keep hold of Sammy, said a voice in his ear – it was the voice of his grandfather, long since dead and buried. He kicked violently, still holding on to Sammy's thin arm. He realised now that the boat had overturned and was weighing him down, trapping him. He could not breathe. His chest was burning.

Then something pulled him further down into the water. It seemed as though Sammy was dragging him to the bottom of the river. Alfie struggled. That ghostly voice was still in his ear so he never relaxed his grip on Sammy's arm. But with his free hand he clawed desperately at the water that was drowning him.

It was no good, though. They were sinking further and further down into the muddy depths of the Thames.

And then, quite suddenly, they shot up again. They were free of the heavy wooden boat and ahead of them were the lights of the houses on the north bank of the river. Alfie gasped for air and Sammy was doing the same. Something was towing them along. No, not something, but someone – Jack.

Jack was a great swimmer. Even with only one arm free, he managed to pull Alfie and Sammy several yards closer to the shore before diving underwater again. Alfie realised that their safety depended on keeping hidden so he took in a deep breath and dived also, towing Sammy with him.

The next time they surfaced, they were quite near the north shore. Sammy was gasping and spluttering, but he was alive.

Well done, lad, Alfie seemed to hear, in his grandfather's voice. He took in a deep breath and looked around. A pitch torch flamed from a metal holder, lighting up the water. Jack, swimming vigorously with one arm and holding Sammy with the other, steered away from this, going upstream towards the Tower of London. Alfie followed, doing his best to keep up with his cousin's strong strokes.

When Jack next paused they were not near to any gas lamp or pitch torch. A few lights came from houses where candles were burning on window sills, but that was not what Alfie focused on. It was something far more puzzling.

A faint ghostly light seemed to be coming from a hole below the river bank. Its grey illumination spilled out over the water – just a glimmer because of the fog – but enough for Jack. Immediately he began to swim in that direction.

It was not easy to swim that way. A slight current

seemed to be pushing them in the opposite direction – forcing them back out into the centre of the river. It was not much, but Alfie was so exhausted that for a moment he was angry with Jack. What did it matter where they landed? Why swim against a current?

And then suddenly he understood. Water was flowing out of a tunnel on the bank. This must be another one of those underground rivers that the sewers drained into. Alfie felt new life flood into his legs and he kicked out energetically. With hope giving him courage, Alfie was surprised how quickly they reached the tunnel. It was quite shallow in there and after a few strokes, they all stood up in the tunnel entrance.

'Next time you want to pull my arms out of the sockets, just ask politely,' said Sammy amiably, rubbing his shoulders.

'Think yourself lucky that you're not feeding the fishes,' retorted Alfie and then remembered that he had last used the expression before Charlie died.

'Poor Charlie – he's dead,' said Jack sadly. 'That bullet blew a hole in his head. I just looked around and saw it, just a second before the boat overturned. I'll miss him. He was a very nice man. Got a family too. A wife and three children.'

'We'll get the men that done it,' said Alfie angrily.

'Let's get to Inspector Denham as fast as we can.'

'Where are we now?' asked Sammy.

'I'd say that it's the Walbrook River,' said Jack after a moment's thought. 'Old Jemmy told me about it – it's the one that comes out near to the Tower of London.'

'Let's get moving,' said Alfie impatiently. 'We'll freeze to death if we hang around here. We'll go up it as far as we can and with a bit of luck we can get out somewhere.'

'According to old Jemmy,' said Jack, 'a man could go anywhere in London and never show his face over ground. The old buried rivers and sewers are like lanes – they all join into each other – that's what old Jemmy used to say, poor old fellow.'

'Funny, wasn't it, Alfie,' said Sammy, wading through the sludgy water as confidently as he walked down Bow Street, 'that story of Mick's. Mick thought he saw the dead body of Jemmy pop up from a sewer!'

'Mick the Drink – that's what Grandad used to call him! Who cares what he . . .' said Alfie impatiently and then stopped. A sudden idea had come to him. He turned it over in his mind as he sloshed through the water, his arm firmly holding Sammy's elbow.

'Jack,' he said slowly. 'Do you remember when you was telling me that Jemmy never drank? Why was that again?'

'Because he used to drink too much when he was younger.' Jack sounded surprised at Alfie's sudden interest.

'No, the bit about his aunt and about his twin brother.'

'That's right, his parents died when he was only seven and one of his mother's sisters took him and the other aunt took his brother Ned. He never saw his brother again. He used to say that he, Jemmy that is, had terribly bad luck. It was the wrong aunt that adopted him, that's what he used to say. Very bitter about it, he was.'

'No, he didn't have much luck, did he, poor old Jemmy,' observed Sammy.

'That man from the post office seemed to think that it wasn't the raiders killed him,' said Alfie, plodding on down the tunnel. It was funny how after a while you got used to the stink and to the slime under your feet, he thought philosophically. You got used to the darkness, too. He had begun to make out the roof and the walls of the tunnel. 'Did you hear him, Sam?' he asked. 'Bristly Eyebrows, I mean. Did you hear him say that?'

'I heard him,' said Sammy.

'But —' began Alfie.

'Let's turn to the left here,' interrupted Jack. 'This looks a good big tunnel and it might bring us out near the Tower of London. There's bound to be a manhole somewhere near there so we can climb out.'

'I vote we keep down here as long as possible,' said Sammy. 'It's warmer here than outside. My clothes are beginning to dry a bit and the water don't seem too deep. I'm getting used to the stink now.'

'Why not? If we just keep going straight ahead we should get to somewhere around Drury Lane,' said Jack. 'Should take a couple of hours – it's slow walking in these places but it's not somewhere the raiders will be searching. People don't like these sewers – don't mind them myself. They're nice and warm and they'll be even warmer later on when all the rich folk have their baths and the scullery maids throw down the scrubbing water. Beats going out in a boat, Bert the Tosher used to say. I don't suppose I'll be going out in a boat again, with poor old Charlie dead,' he added in a low voice.

'But what did you think about what Bristly Eyebrows said, Sammy? Do you think that he was telling a lie when he said that the raiders had nothing to do with Jemmy's death?' persisted Alfie. He didn't want to think about Charlie too much at the moment. It was better to keep his mind on the puzzle of Jemmy's death. 'You heard the man. Did you think that he was telling the truth?'

Sammy was silent for a moment and then in a posh voice he said, '*No, nobody touched Jemmy. I saw him myself, after the raid, when I was going home. He was talking to one of the engineers from Birmingham, the fellows that were examining the pump for the fountains.* That's what he said, wasn't it?'

'That's it,' said Alfie with a grin. Sammy had got the man's voice just right. Alfie had forgotten how startled he had sounded, and how his voice had become quite definite when he said that Jemmy was still alive after the raid was over. 'But then,' said Alfie, puzzled, 'how come we found Jemmy's body *before* the raid on the post office?'

There was one other little bit of information at the back of his mind, but somehow he could not locate it. It was something significant, something that happened when he and Jack were hiding in the inn's cellar. He tried to uncover it, but then he decided not to think any more about it for the moment. His first job was to get to Inspector Denham and report what had happened to Charlie and where the robbers – no, *murderers* – were to be found. He was impatient to claim the reward and then . . .

And then he could put all his energies into solving the mystery of Jemmy's death.

CHAPTER 22

JACK-IN-A-BOX

After Tom and Sarah returned from the river that night, the boy was in such a state that she hesitated to leave him alone in Bow Street. They stood in Trafalgar Square under a gas lamp with Mutsy at their feet, while Sarah tried to decide what to do.

'They're all dead,' Tom kept saying despairingly. 'They're all dead. Jack and Alfie and Sammy, they're all dead. I'll be on my own for the rest of my life. I might as well kill myself now and get it over and done with.'

For a while Sarah wondered whether she should offer to stay with him, but that might mean losing her job. Dora could only cover up for her for a short time. If she wasn't at the inn first thing in the morning, questions would be asked. Her absence during the night would be discovered and she would be dismissed.

'Come back with me,' she said eventually. 'I can hide you and Mutsy in the cellar at the inn. No one goes near it in the morning.'

It was lucky, she thought, as she silently ushered him down the passageway to the cellar door, that she had taken the bunch of keys with her.

She managed to find some sacks for Tom to lie on and she left him curled up beside Mutsy, looking very young and very lost. 'Don't you dare stir until I come for you!' she said, and she stole upstairs to bed feeling sick with worry about the three missing boys.

'No one missed you,' said Dora reassuringly as Sarah got into her nightdress. 'Are you all right?'

'Yes,' said Sarah, feeling thankful that Dora sounded so sleepy. In a few minutes the girl was snoring and Sarah was free to think her thoughts and worry about what she was going to do when morning came.

When Dora woke her at seven, she was still half asleep as she scrambled into her clothes and went down the stairs, rubbing her eyes. The Birmingham engineers had not yet appeared but there were a few travellers who wanted to get the early morning stagecoach to Dover and she served them as quickly as she could.

'You take that tray up to the fellow who's supposed to be sick,' she whispered to Dora. 'He gives me the creeps.'

Sarah hardly knew what she was doing as she went up and down the stairs to the kitchen, carrying tray-loads of eggs and rashers of bacon and steaming teapots. She couldn't stop thinking about the missing boys. In a way, they had taken the place of the family that she had never known. They were more like brothers to her than just friends.

Sarah's mother, whoever she was, had dumped her at Coram Fields Foundling Hospital, placing the tiny baby in the crib provided by the charity outside the main door, ringing the bell provided and then disappearing quickly before anyone came to the door.

Most of the babies that were abandoned at this door had been left with something which would identify them if ever the mother was able to reclaim them, but Sarah had nothing – not even clothes. The naked baby had been tucked into the blankets in the crib and left there like an unwanted piece of rubbish. Sarah had no hope that she would ever be retrieved by a mother who seemed to care so little for her daughter.

Sometimes, Sarah envied the boys with their memories of parents, of the grandfather who had loved them all and given them such pieces of wisdom to remember throughout their lives. Mostly, though, she did not allow herself to think about the past, but focused firmly on the future. This morning, however, what with the anxiety about Jack, Alfie and Sammy, and her own exhaustion, she felt near to tears.

'You don't look well, Sarah, girl,' said the innkeeper. 'Why don't you go back to bed? Dora will manage the breakfast – I'll give her a hand if she needs it.' He spoke roughly but he had a very kind heart.

'I'm all right, Mr Pennyfeather,' said Sarah, trying to make her voice sound natural. 'I've just got a bit of a headache. If Dora can manage, would it be all right if I go for a walk in the fresh air?'

'You do that; nothing more for you to do until we start serving lunches. That Birmingham crowd were up so late that they won't show their faces until noon,' said Mr Pennyfeather. 'Stay out as long as you like, or else have a good lie-down on your bed. This has been a hard week with the hours these fellows keep.' And he jerked his thumb upwards towards the bedrooms where the engineers were sleeping.

'Thanks, Mr Pennyfeather,' said Sarah. She almost felt like crying because she was so grateful for this kind treatment. She would definitely stay working at the inn, she thought. None of her mistresses in the fine houses had ever been as kind to her.

Quietly she stole down to the scullery. Kitty was hard at work so Sarah was easily able to take a few cold rashers of bacon and a few uneaten slices of bread from the dirty plates and conceal them under her apron.

Then she went down to the cellar, candle in hand, to release Tom.

To her surprise, he was just beside the door, his face completely white, when she opened it.

'There's a ghost,' he whispered.

'What?' Sarah let the food drop and Mutsy picked it up and neatly swallowed it.

'Listen,' said Tom.

Sarah listened. There was no doubt that there was something – some sound coming from the centre of the cellar, from among the beer barrels.

'Shh,' she said and blew out the candle.

There was a faint glimmer of daylight coming through the cellar window and it was just enough to see Mutsy, shaggy tail waving frantically, making his way through the barrels in the middle of the room.

'Just a rat,' said Sarah reassuringly.

But then there was a creaking sound. Sarah and Tom grasped each other, terrified.

And then a voice.

'Cor blimey, if it isn't old Mutsy,' whispered Alfie.

'So you've turned up again, like three bad pennies,' said Sarah, as Alfie climbed out of the sewer, hoisting up Sammy behind him, followed by Jack. 'What happened to you?' she hissed. 'Tom was scared out of his wits and Mutsy thought that you were dead.'

'We've found the gang's hide-out and they've got the mailbags with them,' said Alfie briefly.

'Poor Charlie Higgins was shot,' said Jack sadly.

'They'd have got us, too,' said Alfie, 'except that Jack had the brains to lead us into the tunnel where one of them underground rivers empties into the Thames. We've been walking through underground sewers and rivers all night. And here we are now, popping up like a jack-in-a-box.'

'Let's get you all out of here,' said Sarah. 'Wait till I see if it's clear and then go as quickly as you can.'

They were in luck. No one was around and in a minute they were all walking briskly down Haymarket.

'You stink!' said Sarah, wrinkling her nose. 'You'd better have a wash and change your clothes before you go to the police station.'

'Not now,' said Alfie decisively. 'We don't want to hang about. What time is it?'

158

'Don't kn—' began Sarah and then at the clang of the bell from St Martin's church, she said, 'That must be half eight.'

'We'll wash our legs in the fountain,' said Alfie as they went along. 'C'mon lads, can't have the Lady Sarah turning up her nose at us.'

'It's probably just our feet and legs that stink, Sarah,' said Sammy.

'The water wasn't deep and it wasn't too bad after the flood a few days ago,' explained Jack as they waded through the fountain and came out shivering.

'So where are the raiders now?' Sarah lowered her voice and spoke into Alfie's ear, but he shuddered and looked around him without reply. He could only think about getting to the police station as soon as possible.

'The jewellers in Hatton Garden have raised the reward to fifteen pounds,' Inspector Denham was just saying to his sergeant when the door burst open and five children and one large muddy dog tumbled into the police station.

'Sir,' gasped Alfie, 'I've got such news for you.'

'What's the matter?' asked the inspector, half-smiling as Mutsy politely wagged his tail and sat down just next to the inspector's well-polished boots with the air of someone handing over responsibility.

'We know where the gang are hiding out,' said Alfie triumphantly. 'The post office raiders' gang.'

'Come into my office,' said Inspector Denham. He seemed almost as excited as Alfie, thought Sarah, as they all followed the inspector. Even Mutsy trailed in, seated himself beside the fire and listened with grave interest to Alfie's story.

When it came to the bit about Charlie Higgins's death, Jack put his hand in front of his face and Alfie's voice quivered for a moment. But the inspector jumped to his feet and opened the door to the outer office.

'Constable, fetch a cab. I'll go straight to Scotland Yard.'

It took only a few minutes for the cab to arrive, but Inspector Denham had thought the whole matter through by then. Sarah said that she had to go back to work, and the sergeant and constable were told to escort Jack, Tom and Mutsy to the cellar in Bow Street, and if necessary to take any suspicious characters into the police station for questioning. Alfie would ride in the cab to Scotland Yard and tell the whole story on the way.

'And you trust this boy?' The room at Scotland Yard was full of policemen, some in plain clothes, others dressed in uniform. Alfie had found it best to keep his eyes fixed on

Inspector Denham while he told the story of how the men in the galley had pulled up the mail bags that had been attached to iron chains.

'Probably had those chains in place before the robbery,' one plain clothes policeman had observed. He had a clever look, thought Alfie. Not like those constables at Bow Street who all looked stupid. For a moment, Alfie wondered whether there was any chance of him joining Scotland Yard when he grew up. He would enjoy it, he thought.

Inspector Denham looked at home with them as he nodded in reply to the suggestion. Just as he had done when asked whether he believed Alfie. A man of few words, but Alfie trusted him more than any of the other policemen there.

When Alfie came to the part where Charlie Higgins had been gunned down, there was a murmur of anger throughout the room. The man who looked like the chief of Scotland Yard – he was the one that was giving all the orders and asking most of the questions – quickly jumped to his feet and barked a few orders. Men started to stream out of the room and into a wide-open space at the end of the passageway. There was a large table there and on it was spread an armoury of guns: rifles and pistols, thought Alfie, half-hoping that he might be given one.

'It's time for you to go, Alfie,' said Inspector Denham

firmly. 'You've done your work; you must leave the rest to us.'

Alfie thought fast. He didn't want to be left behind. 'Best if I go with you, sir,' he said earnestly. 'You might miss the house. Very confusing, all those old places down there in the docks.'

There was a slight hesitation at that. Everyone left in the room looked at one other.

'It might be . . .' said one man, looking at another. They nodded wisely at each other. Inspector Denham started to look unsure.

'Could sit well out of the way . . . on the floor of the boat . . . no danger . . .' This was the chief at Scotland Yard speaking, the geezer that had given all the orders. Alfie began to feel hopeful.

'The boy is right. We have to target the correct house instantly,' said a tough-looking policeman. He shut one eye, aimed a rifle at the portrait of Queen Victoria and then put it into its holster quickly when he saw the chief superintendent's eye upon him.

'Well, sit by me and keep out of trouble; I don't want to have to explain to that dog of yours how you got a hole in your middle,' said Inspector Denham and Alfie gave a polite laugh at the joke.

There were two steamboats waiting by the river's edge

when they got down the Whitehall Stairs. The fog had lifted a little and a few rays of watery sunshine lit up the clock tower at Westminster.

Alfie had never been in a steamboat before and he couldn't believe the speed with which it took off. Under Hungerford Bridge in a minute, then under Waterloo Bridge, and a minute later beneath the iron bridge of Southwark. Before Alfie had even had time to feel nervous, they shot beneath the stone arch of London Bridge and then past the Tower of London. Now Alfie began to feel the palms of his hands getting damp. They were not far from the spot where poor Charlie Higgins had been shot and killed. Their boat was ahead now, and the other steamboat lurked at a little distance.

Waiting for me to give the word, thought Alfie, sitting up a little straighter. The thought of Charlie Higgins gave him courage, strengthened his determination to get the men who shot the unfortunate fisherman so casually. Which was the house? Yes, it was that one. He remembered the broken shutters, one hanging loose in the wind. Confidently he pointed and immediately he felt Inspector Denham's hand on his head, pushing down hard, forcing him to duck down between the seats.

A policeman in front of the boat had taken up a loud hailer and was speaking into it, his voice booming around the water and bouncing off the old wooden houses on Jacob's Island.

'You are surrounded by armed policemen! Give up and come out with your hands above your head!' The words must have been heard on both sides of the river. Alfie wished that he could sit up and see the people coming to the banks.

But there was no answer and no sound from the house with the broken shutters. Peering from under Inspector Denham's knee, Alfie could see a woman with a baby in her arms come to the window of the house next to it. A small boy with a mass of straw-coloured hair, as untidy as a rook's nest and dressed only in a man's ragged jacket which reached to his toes, came out onto the wooden wharf and stared at the steamboat and the armed policemen within it.

'Come out peacefully with your hands raised!' repeated the man with the loud hailer.

Again there was no movement or sound from the house. Alfie began to wonder whether the raiders had already left.

'I will count to ten and then we fire,' announced the loud hailer. And then, slowly, loudly, the count began.

'One, two, three . . .'

A woman in rags rushed, screaming, out of one of the

other houses, seized the small boy by his hair, slapped him hard and dragged him inside.

'. . . four, five, six, seven, eight . . .' Now the count was going more quickly. From all around the boat came the *click-clack* sound of guns being loaded. Inspector Denham pressed hard onto Alfie's head. Alfie went flat on the floorboards of the boat, wriggled under the inspector's knees and had popped up his head by the time the last number was called.

Instantly the police began to fire, the men aiming at the loose shutters and shattering the half-rotten wood. The boat was full of the smell of gunpowder. Alfie turned his face away to avoid sneezing and saw that the other police boat had gone over to the south shore and was now advancing towards the back of Jacob's Island.

Alfie was not the only one who had seen this manoeuvre. The police in his boat began firing even more fiercely, one man taking up position in the front of the boat while another retired to reload his gun. Those with pistols examined them carefully, checking the ball, closing one eye and squinting along the barrel. They were giving cover to the men in the other boat, thought Alfie, admiring the cleverness of it all.

And then three shots rang out from the house. A shower of bullets came back. They were well-armed, these men. Alfie tried to sit up a bit straighter. He wanted to be able to see the gun battle. He would have fun describing it to Sammy later on.

'Get down,' hissed Inspector Denham and he himself ducked as a shot came whizzing over their heads.

'Missed!' called one of the armed policemen. He sounded like he was enjoying himself – rather like the men who went out ratting, thought Alfie.

Then came another shot. This time there was a scream from the front of the boat. The policeman in the prow had been hit. His hands shot into the air. He swung sideways. Another policeman grabbed him; eased him to the floor of the boat.

And then the guns rang out, with shot following shot. All aimed high, Alfie noticed. And soon he saw why.

The wooden wharf surrounded the crazily tilting houses. And around the corner from the end house a black figure, a policeman, advanced, followed by another and another. The shots from the first boat continued to ring out; splintering the walls of the old house and making neat holes appear in the roof. The shutters had been completely shot away now and the glassless windows gaped open into the rooms beyond.

There were no returning shots now.

Suddenly a shout.

'They've escaped!' yelled the boarding party on the wharf.

'Making for a steamer to Holland or some such place,' grunted Inspector Denham in an exasperated voice. 'Get out from under my legs,' he added to Alfie. 'I suppose you're safe now. They've given us the slip!'

Alfie scrambled out and stood up. He looked down the river. There was no sign of the small galley boat that he had seen the night before. Where was it? They had been firing up to a minute before. The men could not have escaped as quickly as that. He looked all around.

Jacob's Island was on a small piece of land surrounded by a ditch. The ancient houses were about three storeys high and on the top floor of each were crazy broken galleries, with poles stretching from gallery to gallery across the swamp, where the unfortunate inhabitants could hang up their sheets to dry – if they had sheets, and ever bothered to wash them.

But today something else hung from these poles! Not sheets, but men! They were trying to cross the river gap between the houses by edging their way across the poles.

'There they are!' yelled Alfie at the top of his voice. And a great shout of joy went up from the policemen in the boat and those on the wharf.

Five men, one wearing a red silk scarf, all of them

murderers and thieves, hung there helplessly from the wooden poles!

A moment after Alfie's shout, the police were pounding up the stairs of the house, guns at the ready, then appearing on the gallery, shouting orders to the men to return.

One dropped down from the pole, falling plop into the water. Quickly two more followed him – all three of them swimming frantically.

It did them no good, though. In a minute Alfie's police boat was beside them, grabbing wrists and knotting rope over them, and pulling them on board like sacks of coal. Alfie felt no pity for them. They had strangled the little post office man and shot poor Charlie Higgins, as well as injuring one of the policemen.

'Come back or we shoot!' called a policeman to the two remaining figures, still hanging from the washing poles, and inch by inch they wriggled back.

'Well,' said Inspector Denham with satisfaction, 'it looks as though we've finally laid hands on Flash Harry, his lieutenants and Sid the Swell himself. I've been waiting for this moment for many a long year.'

CHAPTER 23

MUTSY
PLAYS DETECTIVE

Alfie woke early on Saturday morning. They had gone to bed very late last night, celebrating the successful arrest of Flash Harry and his mob. Inspector Denham had promised to pay over the fifteen pounds on Monday morning and, for once, Alfie had not hesitated to raid the rent box a little in order to provide a celebration supper.

Tom and Jack had gone to sleep soon after the bells of St Paul's had chimed midnight – Tom deliciously full of smoked eel and veal pie and Jack looking very happy that he had persuaded everyone to give five pounds of their reward money to Charlie Higgins's widow for herself and her children.

Alfie and Sammy, however, had stayed awake for a long time, talking over the strange business of the beggar man's body that they had found in Trafalgar Square.

'None of our business, I suppose,' said Sammy, before he went to sleep and Alfie, tired after the excitements of the day, had agreed with him then.

But now Alfie was wide awake and full of energy. He knew that if he did not solve the mystery of Jemmy's death once and for all, it would haunt him in the years to come. 'Curiosity killed the cat,' his mother used to say to him in exasperated tones when he was about three years old, and Alfie had not changed. He had to know the truth about what had happened that night in Trafalgar Square.

He took a mouthful of the pie, a quick swallow from the remains of the beer, wiped his mouth, smoothed down his hair and went to the door.

'Come on, boy,' he said to Mutsy. 'Let's be going.'

The streets were still dark and very foggy when they went out. Mutsy caught a rat lurking among the discarded cabbage stalks in the corner of Covent Garden market and made a good breakfast from it. Alfie strolled along, confident that the dog would overtake him as soon as he had left nothing but a scaly tail lying on the pavement. He was conscious of a great feeling of relief that Flash Harry and Sid the Swell were now behind bars.

When he came to Trafalgar Square, he was joined by Mutsy and they immediately crossed over towards the large statue of King Charles on horseback.

A quick look around was enough to tell him that no one was looking.

Ten minutes later, Alfie surfaced through the hatch in the cellar of the White Horse Inn. He had proved what he suspected. A quick exit from Trafalgar Square to the White Horse Inn could have been made on that fateful night by a man who knew about the underground rivers and sewers of London. There were a few old sacks lying around and he rubbed his own bare feet and legs clean of the traces from the sewer and then did his best with Mutsy's hairy paws.

There was no one around when he reached the top of the cellar steps. Everyone seemed to be at breakfast. Alfie stole up the stairs, followed closely by Mutsy. He knew where he was heading – remembering the scullery maid's words about the dirty boots: *'They're belonging to the gentleman that's sick in bed in number fifteen.'* He paused at the door numbered fifteen and then decided against knocking.

The door handle turned quietly and boy and dog were in the room before the man at the window turned around.

For a second Alfie hesitated. For a second he wondered whether he had made a mistake. This was a gentleman, a gentleman dressed in a good tweed suit with well-polished boots, a heavy silver watch-chain over a well-cut waistcoat, a neatly trimmed ginger beard and moustache.

Mutsy, however, did not hesitate. In an instant he was across the room and had flung himself onto the gentleman with the ginger beard and moustache. The big affectionate dog was so excited that his wagging tail swept a small ornament, a china shepherdess, off a low table by the window. He was panting with excitement as he licked the well-washed hands, twisting his hairy body around the man now known as Ned.

'He's been missing you, Jemmy,' said Alfie quietly. And then as the man opened his mouth, Alfie shook his head at him. 'No good trying to deny it, Jemmy. You've said it yourself often enough. A dog always knows his friends. He never forgets.'

The man who was called Ned sat down heavily on a chair by the window.

'How did you guess?' he asked.

'Guessed something was wrong as soon as I saw the body,' boasted Alfie. 'I noticed that the cheeks and the neck were shaved and that the beard was trimmed. Never knew you to be so fussy about things like that, Jemmy.'

'Was that all?' Jemmy stared at Alfie.

'Let me tell you what happened.' Alfie was enjoying himself. He liked that look of respect in Jemmy's eye. He carefully replaced the china shepherdess on the table and sat down on the rug in front of the window. Mutsy lay down beside him, placed his heavy head on Alfie's knee and wagged his tail again at Jemmy.

'Jack told me that you had a twin brother called Ned. You was adopted by one aunt and he by another,' began Alfie.

'He had all the luck,' said Jemmy bitterly. 'The aunt that adopted him got married and moved to Birmingham. She and her husband didn't have any children of their own so they gave Ned a good education and he became an engineer and was called by their name, Batson.'

'And he told you all that when you met in Trafalgar Square that night. Who recognised who first?'

'I recognised him; he didn't want anything to do with me,' said Jemmy angrily. 'But he couldn't deny it. We were always like two peas out of a pod. Our own mother could hardly tell us apart. And there he was walking past me in his fancy clothes and even after I told him who I was – well, he was just looking through me, like I was a piece of dirt.'

'You asked him for money, of course.' Jemmy would

ask anyone for money. That was the way that he lived.

'And he refused!' Jemmy's voice was choked with anger. 'He had neither kith nor kin, lived by himself in a big house – boasted about it – and about all the money that he had.'

'And you lost your temper and punched him.' That would be the way of it, thought Alfie. Jemmy had a terrible temper.

'I never meant to do it . . . got an awful shock when I found he was dead . . . I just punched him, but he fell hard against that statue and hit his head.'

'And then you got the bright idea of changing clothes with him.' So I was right when I said to the constable that it was the stone horse that done it, thought Alfie.

Jemmy gave a reluctant grin. 'Didn't think of that at first,' he admitted. 'When no one was looking, I got the manhole cover open, dropped down into it to make sure that Bert the Tosher wasn't around and then dragged the body after me. I had a bit of a search around his pockets for any loose change or bank notes or anything like that and then I found the key to this room here. Big label it had on it. *Room number 15; if found, return to the landlord of the White Horse Inn.* That started to give me ideas. Thought I'd have a few days at the inn and if that worked out, if no one suspected me, well . . .' Jemmy faced Alfie defiantly. 'I thought I might just turn my life around, live respectable – do something with myself.'

'So you turned yourself into Ned.' Alfie stood up, took a quick look out of the window and then sat down again. There was no sign of the stagecoach yet.

'How did you guess about the sewer?' asked Jemmy again.

'I noticed the manhole, just beside the statue of the horse and the king, and I guessed the sewer was under there. There were lumps of ice around the body as if water had run off it, as if it had got very wet, but there had been no rain that night – just frost and fog – so the body must have been in water. And old Mick said he saw Jemmy come up from hell.'

'What are you going to do? I'll kill you if you try to tell anyone.' Jemmy stood up abruptly.

'And, of course, you knew all about the sewers and the underground rivers,' continued Alfie calmly. He did not take much notice of Jemmy's threat. Mutsy would not let Jemmy lay a finger on his master. 'You told Jack all about them,' he continued. 'You probably knew all about that hatch in the cellar of the White Horse Inn – when you worked on the sewers you would have seen rubbish being thrown down there. You would have known that you could hide in the sewers until most people in the inn had gone to bed and then get quietly into number fifteen without anyone seeing you.'

'That's right,' admitted Jemmy. 'I decided that I would pretend to be ill – have a sore throat. I didn't see myself talking with that Birmingham accent.'

'Should have cleaned your boots a bit better; the boot boy was complaining about them. That gave me another clue.'

'It was one of them interfering maids took them. I just lay down and pulled the blankets over my head or looked away when they came in. Just muttered at them.'

'Hard to get the smell of the sewer out of boots. Should have tied them around your neck. The trouble with you, Jemmy, is that you couldn't wait to be a proper gent,' said Alfie in a friendly way. 'Couldn't fool Mutsy, though, could you?' he added as he rose to his feet and went to the door, his hand on the dog's collar.

Jemmy's eyes followed him. 'What are you going to do?' he asked and his voice was suddenly hoarse.

Alfie didn't reply, but opened the door and stood for a moment, looking back. 'Glad it was an accident, though. Jack thinks a lot of you and so does Mutsy.'

'Will you tell the police?' The man's face looked strained.

Alfie gave a reassuring grin. 'The jewel robbery is

solved,' he said 'and that's all that they were interested in.'
He watched the look of relief come over the man's face,
and, in a slightly louder voice, he said, 'Have a good trip,
sir.'

Then Alfie, with Mutsy at his heels like a well-trained
servant, swept down the stairs, past the landlord, past the
engineers and out on to Haymarket.

'C'mon, Mutsy,' he said. 'I think a promising young
Scotland Yard detective like yourself deserves a good
breakfast.'

He wouldn't go to the ordinary breakfast stalls along
the Strand or around Covent Garden, he decided. He and
Mutsy needed a man's place, a place that would be fitting
for a pair that had solved a mystery that baffled the top
policeman in Bow Street and all the best brains at
Scotland Yard. He knew just the place to go to.

He turned down Orange Street and there it was in
front of him: the Racquet and Handle. Painted a deep
midnight blue with the decorations picked out in gold, it
was one of the most splendid public houses in the area.

Inside, the place was dimly lit by a single gas lamp, but
there was a delicious smell of fried eggs, rashers of bacon,
herrings, black pudding, slices of beef and hot muffins.
Most of the polished dark oak tables were occupied by
toffs on their way to work, each with a starched white

napkin tucked under his chin, but there was one table empty in a dark corner near to the fire.

Mutsy discreetly disappeared under the table while Alfie sat down and took up a menu card.

'Yes?' The waiter didn't look too happy. But then he noticed the silver shilling that Alfie had carefully placed in the centre of the table. 'Yes, sir?' he said more respectfully. 'See something you fancy, sir?'

Alfie scanned the long list and then put the card down. 'I'll have two of everything on the breakfast menu,' he said. 'I need to keep my strength up with the job that I have.' From under the table, against his bare leg, he could feel an emphatic wag from a hairy tail.

'Oh, and one of them napkins,' he added as the waiter moved away. He sat up very straight, feeling the warmth of Mutsy's head on his bare feet. He fancied the life of those toffs with the napkins, he thought. Perhaps he would be a toff himself one day. Start off as an ordinary copper, work his way up to Scotland Yard, wear a smart suit, have breakfast in the Racquet and Handle, carry a pistol in his back pocket.

And wherever he went, everyone would call him 'sir'.

ACKNOWLEDGEMENTS

Many thanks to my agent Peter Buckman of Ampersand Agency and to my editor Anne Clark, both of whom have helped me to tighten up the narrative of this, the fifth 'Alfie' book.

Thanks are also due to the team at Piccadilly and to family and friends.

THE LONDON MURDER MYSTERIES

The MONTGOMERY MURDER

The police must move fast to catch the killer of
wealthy Mr Montgomery. They need an insider, someone streetwise, cunning, bold . . . someone like Alfie.
When Inspector Denham makes him an offer, Alfie
and his gang must sift clues, shadow suspects and
negotiate a sinister world of double-dealing and danger.

The DEADLY FIRE

A man's body lies in the burnt-out
wreckage of the Ragged School.
The police say the fire was just an accident –
but Alfie suspects foul play.
Determined to find out the truth, Alfie and his gang
must follow up each clue, investigate every suspect and
risk their lives on the dangerous streets of Victorian
London – until the ruthless murderer is caught.

THE LONDON MURDER MYSTERIES

MURDER ON STAGE

A scream rings out through the theatre. The man on stage is dead! Who killed him? Alfie has a few suspects in his sights. But when the spotlight turns on Alfie himself, the search for the murderer becomes a fight for his own survival.

DEATH OF A CHIMNEY SWEEP

Alfie knew who it was the moment he saw the body under the gas lamp. Joe the chimney sweep. No one else seems to care about the death of a poor boy, but Alfie has reason to believe that Joe was murdered. So he and his gang will risk their lives on the rooftops of London and brave the dark, dangerous world of the chimney sweeps, until they uncover the deadly truth.

Coming soon

THE LONDON MURDER MYSTERIES

DEATH IN DEVIL'S ACRE

Alfie and his gang are on a dangerous mission.

Spying on a Russian secret agent, they must be quick, clever and totally invisible. It's a thrilling game, until the Russian is found murdered, and Alfie faces the greatest threat of his life . . .

SAXBY SMART
PRIVATE DETECTIVE
SIMON CHESHIRE

Be the sleuth yourself and crack all the cases!

In each story Saxby Smart – schoolboy detective – gives you, the reader, clues which help solve the mystery. Are you 'smart' enough to find the answers?

The Curse of the Ancient Mask

A mysterious curse, suspicious sabotage of a school competition, and a very unpleasant relative all conspire to puzzle Saxby Smart, schoolboy private detective.

Stories include: *The Curse of the Ancient Mask*, *The Mark of the Purple Homework* and *The Clasp of Doom*.

The Hangman's Lair

A terrifying visit to the Hangman's Lair to recover stolen money, a serious threat of blackmail, and a mystery surrounding a stranger's unearthly powers test Saxby to the limit in this set of case files!

Stories include: *The Hangman's Lair*, *Diary of Fear* and *Whispers from the Dead*.

www.saxbysmart.co.uk

THE LONDON MURDER MYSTERIES

www.piccadillypress.co.uk/ londonmurdermysteries

Head online to find out more
about Alfie's world!